C000121729

COCONUT CHOCOLATE MURDER

A MAPLE HILLS COZY MYSTERY #7

WENDY MEADOWS

1

Nikki hummed sweetly as she took inventory of the chocolates resting in the front display case. Feeling pretty in the blue autumn dress she had purchased the day before, she hoped that Hawk would pay her a compliment when he dropped in for lunch. "This is lovely," Nikki murmured, smiling and hugging a wooden clipboard to her chest as she admired the window display. Walking away from the front counter, she made her way to the front door and looked outside. Autumn leaves were playing in a crisp, cold wind. The days were getting shorter and colder. The landscape surrounding the town was blossoming with bright colors falling from the eyes of a sleepy autumn morning. Nikki was in love.

Drawing a deep breath of chocolate, peppermint, and coffee, she smiled and watched the leaves dance across the empty street. Glad to be at the store before Lidia and Nikki arrived, Nikki cherished the time alone. She loved her new family very deeply—but standing alone in her store, she watched the autumn morning whisper gentle promises of days filled with strolls in warm sweaters and chilly nights huddled around a campfire with hot cocoa. Nikki also cherished this solitary, quiet time. "So lovely," she whispered.

Closing her eyes, Nikki walked ahead in time until she arrived in a snowy, cozy little Vermont town covered with icicles and children building snowmen. She imagined smoke coming from warm fireplaces attached to cozy homes filled with laughter and love; she saw the smoke rising up into a winter sky dropping strange and wonderful snow down onto the world. Then Nikki saw herself walking with Hawk, hand in hand, down the sidewalk toward her store, sipping hot cocoa, talking, and laughing. "Time to rest," Nikki told herself. "No more cases. Time to work on my book, spend time in my store, and rest."

Opening her eyes, Nikki smiled. Outside she saw a grumpy Mr. Wipinski stroll past her store toward his own shop. The old man was holding a brown cup of coffee in one hand and a newspaper in the other. "Good thing I declined the job at the paper," Nikki giggled sweetly. "Mr. Wipinski isn't one of my biggest fans."

Sighing, she returned to the front counter and continued with her inventory. As she worked, the autumn winds outside filled her store with music. Outside, two vicious eyes appeared across the street and looked at Nikki's store. Two furious hands tugged on a gray coat, whispered a low threat, and walked away just as Lidia pulled down the Main Street and swung her car into a parking space next to Nikki's SUV.

"Morning, dear," Lidia said, walking into the store wearing a thick, heavy, brown coat.

Nikki turned and took a look at Lidia's coat. "My, you look like you're ready to go explore the North Pole in that!"

Lidia locked the front door behind her and then turned to Nikki. "I'm not a cold-weather person," she replied, smelling the coffee roaming through the air like a warm, welcoming friend. "*The Farmer's Almanac* is calling for penetrating cold and blizzard-like conditions this winter."

"How cozy," Nikki beamed. "We didn't get much snow in Georgia."

Lidia took off her coat, revealing a yellow sweater hanging over a thick, gray, woolen dress, and placed it on a wooden coat rack next to the front door. "Dear, let me explain something very carefully to you. Winters in Vermont, especially northern Vermont, are nothing to sneeze at. The windchill factor alone can steal a person's body heat within minutes. And as far as the snow is concerned, let me tell you, it's pretty at first, but then it becomes a serious hazard. You have to continually dig out your car in the morning, be careful on the roads...and the children and their snowballs!"

Nikki giggled at the frown on Lidia's face. "That bad, huh?"

"Little rascals love to ambush you," Lidia fussed and hurried away to the back office. After making herself a cup of coffee, she joined Nikki at the front counter. "Our business will cool down this winter, too. Not many people in the market for chocolate when it's freezing outside. Autumn is our last drizzle to bring in some dough."

Nikki bit her bottom lip. "I've been thinking, partner."

Lidia calmly sipped her coffee. "I figured as much," she told Nikki. "You want to run a hot chocolate shop during the winter, right? You want to offer different flavors of chocolate—Nikki Bates' homemade versions, of course—and even toss in a bookshelf or two and a couple of cozy reading chairs and café tables."

Nikki's eyes grew wide. "How did you know that, Lidia?"

Lidia smiled. "Because I've been thinking the same thing. Listen, partner, if we move some of the display shelves into storage during the winter, we'll have just enough room to transform the main floor into a cozy seating area. The back counter is perfect for making hot cocoa. We can even make some pastries. I was thinking we could offer—prepare yourself—chocolate muffins."

Nikki loved the idea and hugged Lidia happily.

"When the snow arrives, we'll be ready," Lidia promised with a warm smile.

"I can't wait for the snow," Nikki said excitedly. "I may even throw a snowball of my own." She winked.

"I thought as much," Lidia winked back at her. "Oh, speaking of children, here comes our dear little Tori."

Tori unlocked the front door and stepped inside the warm shop. "Good morning," she said sweetly. Taking off a thin, pink coat, Tori quickly pirouetted in the pink and white polka-dotted dress she was wearing. "I know the dress is old fashioned," she blushed, "but I fell in love with it the moment I saw it."

Nikki gently brushed Tori's bangs away from her eyes. "You look beautiful, honey."

"Like a princess," Lidia chimed in.

Tori blushed some more. Smelling the coffee in the air, she looked toward the back office. "I think I will have some coffee."

Nikki and Lidia watched Tori walk away. "Too bad Zach put the lodge up for sale and moved to Minnesota," Nikki said. "Those two made a sweet couple."

Lidia sighed. "There's a good man out there waiting for our Tori. We have to work on her self-esteem more, though. Still, I think she's much stronger now."

Nikki agreed. "Tori is no push-over. She's not going to be sweet-talked by any two-cent loser, that's for sure."

"Speaking of romance," Lidia turned to Nikki and grinned, "when is Hawk going to place a ring on your finger?"

Now it was time for Nikki to blush. "Oh, Lidia," she said and hurried away to finish her inventory.

2

L ater, when the store opened, the person wearing the gray coat stepped into Nikki's store. Cynthia Grove marched up to the front counter. "Nikki Bates," she hissed.

Nikki carefully slid a tray of peppermint chocolate into the front display case and straightened up. "Hello, Mrs. Grove," she said, forcing her voice to be pleasant. "How are you this morning?"

Cynthia stared at Nikki, her hateful, gray eyes and thin lips giving her face an almost skeletal appearance. Nikki found the woman repulsive. Maybe it was the way she kept her dark gray hair tied up in a tight bun? Or maybe it was the drab, colorless dresses she wore that cried out depression? Or maybe, Nikki thought—dismissing her earlier opinions—it was the hate spilling out from a pair of poisonous eyes and coming from a hollow, bitter heart. "So the governor came here and personally congratulated you, did he?" asked Mrs. Grove. "You, who forced disgrace on my sister and her husband."

"The governor wished to thank me for helping solve a case involving some very dangerous, corrupt men," Nikki explained in a calm voice. "As far as disgracing your sister and her husband, you're very wrong, Mrs. Grove. The mayor of our town was a criminal."

Nikki's words caused Cynthia to explode. "How dare you! Because of you, my sister suffered a mental breakdown. I had to hire a full-time caretaker for her."

Nikki braced herself. "Mrs. Grove, please leave my store if you can't talk calmly to me."

"Calmly," Cynthia hissed. "Listen to me, I'm going to make you suffer for your crimes against my sister and her husband. Everything was fine until you showed up."

Lidia and Tori stepped out of the back office. Nikki shook her head at them. "It's okay, girls. Mrs. Grove was just leaving."

"Before I do," Cynthia snapped at Nikki, "I want a piece of peppermint chocolate. My cleaning lady needs a snack."

Nikki rolled her eyes. Taking a piece of brown parchment paper from a box on the counter, she bent down and retrieved a square of peppermint chocolate. "On the house," she told Cynthia.

Cynthia snatched the confection out of Nikki's right hand. "I hope she doesn't vomit after eating this garbage," she snapped and walked away.

Nikki, Lidia, and Tori watched Cynthia leave the store and go toward the main square a couple of blocks up the street. "That woman never set well with me," Lidia told Nikki. "She has more money than she has sense. Her husband was a very wealthy man whom people respected.

Why Mr. Grove married a venomous spider like Cynthia, I'll never know."

"Cynthia probably blackmailed him," Tori said in a serious voice. Even though she didn't mean to be funny, Nikki and Lidia both began to laugh.

"Come on, girls, we've got work to do," Nikki laughed, pushing Cynthia's threat from her mind.

The rest of the morning went calmly. A few customers drifted in, purchased some chocolate, and drifted back out into the wind and faded away. Hawk wandered into the store around lunchtime. "Hello, ladies," he said, munching on a carrot.

Nikki and Lidia were talking about how they were going to transform the center of the shop into a seating area for the hot cocoa café when he walked in. They both stopped talking and smiled. "Well, Hawk Daily, are you wearing a suit and tie?" Lidia asked, shocked.

Hawk looked down at the shiny pair of black shoes he was wearing. He didn't mind wearing the gray suit, but the shoes were torturing his feet. "I feel silly," he complained, "but you know how Pop is. He insisted I look my best for Mr. Fancy Lawyer."

"Speaking of lawyers," Nikki said, admiring how handsome Hawk looked in his suit, "how did everything go?"

Hawk finished his carrot. "Where's number three?" he asked.

"Oh, Tori went down to the diner for an early lunch,

and then she's going home to study. Slow morning," Nikki admitted.

Hawk examined the cozy chocolate shop. "You know, if you moved some of the shelves out, you could maybe turn this place into a coffee shop for the winter."

Nikki and Lidia looked at each other and laughed. "We were thinking more along the lines of a hot chocolate shop," Nikki explained.

"If you girls need an investor, I might just be the guy," Hawk told them. "My Aunt Frawly," he said, "left me quite a bit of the green stuff. I didn't even know the woman. I mean, I saw her a few times growing up, but that was it. To be honest, she was a bit creepy." Hawk rubbed the back of his neck.

Lidia nudged Nikki with her elbow. "Better marry this man before the women in this town find out he's rich."

Nikki blushed and quickly changed the subject. "Why are you eating a carrot?"

"Huh?" Hawk asked. "Oh, uh...well, after I met with the lawyer, I went and had an eye examination. I might need reading glasses sometime in the future."

"So you figure eating a carrot will help?" Lidia asked Hawk and rolled her eyes.

"Can't hurt," Hawk said in a serious voice. "I have a whole bag of carrots out in my jeep."

Nikki sighed. She walked up to Hawk and hugged his arm. "Come on, silly, you can buy me lunch since you're now a rich man."

"It'll be my pleasure," Hawk told Nikki and kissed her nose. "Lidia, what can we bring you back from the diner? Lunch is on me."

Nikki looked at Lidia. All of a sudden, her friend seemed very lonely. "Hey," she said, trying to sound casual, "why don't we lock up here and all go to lunch together?"

Hawk caught onto Nikki's suggestion. He could see that Lidia seemed lonely, too. "Two beautiful ladies for lunch? Must be my lucky day."

Lidia hesitated. The fact was, she was lonely. Herbert was away visiting a sick relative in Wyoming. Of course, no one else knew Herbert was out of town. If anyone found out, Lidia knew, they would insist she come and stay with them. Nikki, of course, would be on the top of the list. Perhaps she was being silly, but she didn't want to impose on her friends. "I'm hungry," she finally smiled.

Hawk walked up to Lidia and swung his arm around her frail shoulders. "Take me to the bank, lady," he winked at her.

"Don't tempt me," Lidia grinned back.

Nikki went to retrieve her white jacket, worn more for style than warmth, from the coat rack next to the front door when Chief Daily walked in. "Hello, Chief Daily, we were—" Nikki stopped talking. Something in Chief Daily's eyes sent a horrible feeling screaming into her heart, shattering her peace.

"Cynthia Grove was found dead in her home an hour ago," Chief Daily announced. Reaching into the pocket of his coat, he pulled out a plastic bag holding a square piece of chocolate. Nikki stared at the plastic bag. Leaning forward, she saw that someone had taken a single bite out of the chocolate. Chief Daily looked past Nikki. His eyes were worried and his face red from the strong winds howling outside. "Hawk, Cynthia Grove was poisoned."

3

"**P**oisoned!" Nikki gasped.

Lidia reached out and grabbed Nikki's hand. "How do you know that old bat was poisoned?" Lidia asked Chief Daily.

Chief Daily handed the plastic bag in his hand to Hawk. "Until the chocolate is tested, I don't. I've been a cop for a long time, though. My gut tells me Cynthia Grove died from poisoning."

"Who found the body, Pop?" Hawk asked, examining the chocolate.

"Sam Heatherton, the old lady who cleans Cynthia's house," Chief Daily told Hawk. Then he looked at Nikki. "The chocolate in that bag came from your store, Ms. Bates?"

Nikki nodded. "Cynthia Grove paid me a visit earlier. She was angry and upset with me. She still blames me for the mayor being sent to prison and his wife suffering a mental breakdown. She—"

"That old bat swore to get even with Nikki," Lidia exploded. "But Nikki held her tongue. She even gave Mrs. Grove a free piece of chocolate."

"Cynthia wanted a piece of your chocolate?" Chief Daily asked, confused. "It's a known fact that she doesn't like you living here."

"That old bat was being rude," Lidia said. "She claimed she wanted a piece of chocolate to feed to her cleaning lady."

"I thought Cynthia was being insulting. I didn't want to argue with her or cause a scene in my store, so I gave her a piece of peppermint chocolate, and she left," Nikki explained.

"I see," Chief Daily said and rubbed the bridge of his nose. Dressed in his work uniform, he looked old and tired rather than authoritative and smart. "I won't have any definitive answers until I send the chocolate off to the crime lab downstate. But as it stands right now, Ms. Bates, you, Lidia and the young lady who works here with you are all suspects. I'm afraid I'm going to have to ask you all to come down to the station for questioning."

"I'll call Tori," Lidia said and hurried off to the back office. Chief Daily followed her.

"Oh, Hawk," Nikki said, slowly placing her hands to her mouth.

Hawk opened the plastic bag and sniffed the inside. Detecting a faint scent coming from the chocolate, he nodded his head. "It's something, all right," he told Nikki and closed the bag. "The crime lab will tell us for sure."

"I didn't poison Cynthia Grove," Nikki protested.

"Oh, Nikki, I know that," Hawk said and gently put his arm around her shoulders. "But we do have a murder, and your chocolate was found at the crime scene, kiddo."

Nikki closed her eyes. She listened to the wind howling outside. The temperatures were slowly dropping down into the upper forties. Suddenly, Nikki felt very cold, and the idea of winter approaching scared her. The thoughts of hot chocolate and snowball fights and warm fireplaces seemed sad and lonely rather than warm and comforting. "Hawk, someone in this town hates me more than Cynthia Grove did. Whoever that person is, he or she killed that poor woman to make me suffer."

"Yep," Hawk agreed, drawing in a deep breath. "The only problem is we don't know who that person is. A lot of people here were loyal to the mayor and are very bitter that you exposed him. I hate to admit it, but some people would organize a parade if you were handcuffed and hauled away to prison yourself."

"I know," Nikki said sadly. "I see the looks."

"But," Hawk added, "there's a lot of people in our little town who think you're great, too."

Nikki struggled to smile but failed. "Oh, Hawk!" She threw her face into Hawk's chest and began crying.

"Hey, now, it's okay," Hawk said, gently wrapping his arms around Nikki. "We'll figure out who killed Cynthia Grove, you just wait and see. Ol' Hawk is on the case."

Lidia walked out of the back office with Chief Daily. "Tori is on her way to the station and—" Lidia stopped talking. She saw Nikki crying, cradled in Hawk's arms.

Chief Daily kicked at the floor with his right foot. "I'm

going to make some changes to this town and get the bad eggs out once and for all," he promised. "Until then, I'm afraid this establishment must be closed for investigation."

Lidia looked at Nikki. Then she slowly glanced around the chocolate shop. Her heart broke. "I can't stand it, I just can't stand it," she said as her own tears began to fall. Grabbing her coat, she ran outside.

"Can we eat first?" Nikki asked Hawk, wiping at her tears.

Hawk looked down into Nikki's beautiful, tear-soaked face. "Of course we can," he smiled. "Pop, we'll be over at the diner."

Chief Daily shook his head. "I want Ms. Bates out of sight and out of mind for now," he ordered Hawk. "I'll run over to the diner and get lunch for everyone. As soon as word of Cynthia Grove's death gets loose in this town, a lot of angry people are going to be storming into my office demanding answers. And I think you know how the news about the murder is going to get out, too."

"Sam," Hawk said.

Chief Daily nodded. "That old woman has a tongue laced with grease. I ordered her to keep quiet, but I doubt she will. I predict this town will be ready to light torches and go after Ms. Bates with pitchforks before dinner time."

"Sam will tell people about the chocolate," Hawk said miserably.

"Oh dear," Nikki moaned painfully.

Chief Daily walked up to Nikki and carefully put his hand on her shoulder. "Ms. Bates—Nikki—I know you didn't kill Cynthia Grove. And I intend to find the person who did. But for now, please, I beg you, do as we ask you."

"Of course," Nikki agreed and wiped at her tears. With sad eyes, she looked around her chocolate shop. "Lidia and I were going to change the store into a hot chocolate shop before the first snow arrived..." Unable to say any more, Nikki walked outside.

Lidia was standing out on the front sidewalk hugging her arms. The wind was up, blowing leaves across the empty streets and up against quiet storefronts. "If you dare say you're leaving, I will never forgive you," Lidia told Nikki, staring at a warm bakery across the street. "You're —no, *we*—are fighters, do you hear me?"

Nikki put her arm around Lidia's trembling shoulder. "I'm not going anywhere," she promised. "We still have a hot chocolate shop to create."

Lidia looked into Nikki's teary eyes. "You are an amazing woman, Nikki Bates, and I am proud to be your friend. I'm going to stand by you no matter what. We're both upset and heartbroken right now, but mark my word, in a couple of weeks we'll be back in our store talking about throwing snowballs at each other."

"You're my family, not my friend," Nikki told Lidia and hugged her tightly.

"I know, honey, I know," Lidia replied and hugged Nikki back.

Nikki glimpsed movement across the street. Gently letting go of Lidia, she saw an old man staring at her. "Who is that?" Nikki asked.

Lidia drew her watery eyes across the street. An old man wearing a dark green windbreaker was staring at

Nikki. "Let's go," the old man told a toy fox terrier attached to a blue leash he was holding in his right hand.

Nikki watched the old man walk away and vanish around a street corner. "I've never seen that man before," Lidia said, her brow furrowed, "but he sure seemed interested in you."

4

Hearing Hawk and Chief Daily step outside, Nikki turned and watched Chief Daily close the front door to her chocolate shop. Hawk offered a supportive smile, but his eyes dropped to the sidewalk like wet sand. "Ready, ladies?" he asked.

"Hawk," Nikki said, "an old man was standing across the street staring at me. He was walking a small dog." Nikki pointed to the street corner where the old man had vanished. "He went that way, down Dove Avenue."

"Go," Chief Daily commanded.

Hawk didn't waste another second. He dashed across the street on his long legs. Nikki watched him dash around the street corner with worried eyes. Chief Daily put a warm hand on her shoulder. "Everything is going to be all right, I assure you," he promised Nikki.

Nikki patted Chief Daily's hand. "I know," she said, her voice empty of confidence.

Ten minutes later, Hawk returned empty-handed. Shrugging at Chief Daily, he explained that he couldn't find anyone on Dove Avenue. "I searched over on Pine Street and Peppermint Lane," he added. "The old man you ladies saw must be Houdini."

"Could the man have ventured into any of the stores?" Chief Daily asked Hawk.

"All the stores are closed," Hawk answered. "I checked the doors."

Chief Daily rubbed his chin and looked at Lidia. "You never saw the man before, Lidia?"

Lidia shook her head resolutely. "Not in my life, and I know every face in this town. The old man watching Nikki was a stranger."

"Okay," Chief Daily sighed, "no laws in this town against someone walking a dog and stopping to look at you. We better get on down to the station."

Hawk looked out across the street at the stores that would soon fall into hibernation for the winter. Allowing the wind to wash over his face with cold fingers, he studied the stores with careful eyes as the leaves continued to dance and the sky above slowly began to turn gray. "Pop," he said in a low voice, "I've got a funny feeling on this one."

"Me, too," Chief Daily agreed.

Nikki was surprised that she was able to eat. She was even more surprised to find that she was hungry enough to eat every bite of food on her plate. Standing in Hawk's office near the window, holding a white plate in her hand, she put a bite of delicious turkey in her mouth. "Good," she said.

Lidia and Tori were sitting in two brown chairs Hawk had pulled into his office. Lidia looked down at the turkey dinner sitting on a plate resting on Hawk's desk. "Please eat," Tori begged Lidia.

"Please," Hawk supported Tori. Sitting behind his desk, he worked on a turkey sandwich.

Lidia was hungry. It was just that her stomach was tied in knots. Hesitantly, she grabbed her plate and began to nibble on stuffing. "Happy?" she asked.

"Yes," Hawk told her. "I know you're upset, but you need your strength."

"Yes, dad," Lidia rolled her eyes. "Oh, I'm sorry," she quickly apologized. "I'm worried. That man we saw...he was so creepy."

"Thin gray hair, glasses, green windbreaker, brown pants..." Hawk said, putting down his sandwich. "Not much to go on. Mr. Ross matches that description... so do Mr. Walton and Mr. Gordon. Lidia, those men aren't creepy. Why did the old man you saw raise your eyebrows?"

"It was the way he looked at me," Nikki answered for Lidia. "Very creepy, Hawk."

Tori looked at Lidia. "It's going to be okay."

"I hope so, dear," Lidia tried to smile but failed.

Nikki walked away from the window, put her plate down on Hawk's desk, and folded her arms together. "I'm going to find that man," she announced.

"Oh no, you're not," Hawk objected.

"Yes, I am," Nikki argued, "but, not in the way you're

thinking. Hawk, let me go back to the chocolate shop, and you keep watch from a safe distance. When the man appears—if he appears—grab him."

Hawk considered Nikki's suggestion. "Worth a shot," he agreed and finished off his sandwich. "Lidia, you and Tori stay here in my office."

"No way," Lidia said, putting her plate down. "I'm going with Nikki, and so is Tori. We're a team."

"That's right," Tori added stubbornly.

"You're also two individuals who are under questioning for the murder of Mrs. Grove," Hawk reminded them. "So you either sit here in my office or sit in a jail cell, ladies."

"Stay here," Nikki pleaded with Lidia and Tori. "I have a feeling our missing friend will appear if I'm alone."

Lidia narrowed her eyes at Hawk. "If anything happens to her, mister, you're going to feel my anger."

Hawk held his hands up in the air. "I promise to bring Nikki back in one piece, okay?"

"You better," Tori snapped. "We know where you...uh, work."

Hawk looked at Nikki. "I guess I better bring you back in one piece if I want to make it through this day in one piece."

Nikki felt grateful that Lidia and Nikki cared so much about her. She quickly gave them a hug apiece and left Hawk's office. Walking outside, she paused and took in the beautiful day set before her with a brilliance and color that no poet could place into words. Allowing the cold winds that were exploring the day to touch her face and play in her hair, Nikki closed her eyes.

"Home...sometimes we have to fight for home," she whispered.

Feeling Hawk put his right hand on her shoulder, Nikki opened her eyes. "What are you thinking?" he asked.

Nikki turned around and looked into Hawk's caring, concerned eyes. "I moved to Vermont to begin a new life, Hawk. It would be easy to run back to Georgia, to give up on what I have here in this little town. I never expected to fall in love again and meet people who would become my family. I'm very happy, Hawk...and content. My ex-husband, if he were here, would insist I leave at once. He never liked to rock the boat, as people say." Nikki paused as images of her ex-husband floated into her troubled mind. "What would I do if I left Vermont? Where would I go? This is my home now, Hawk—you, Lidia, Tori—you're all my home."

Hawk gently caressed Nikki's cheek with his hand. "You're going to make it, Nikki," he said softly. "I know right now we've been dropped into another case, but we haven't lost yet, have we? You wait and see, in a few days you'll be back at your shop selling that excellent chocolate you make."

"And then what, Hawk?" Nikki asked, touching his hand. "Will the cases keep coming? Will we ever have peace?"

"Does it really matter? As long as we're together, that's all that matters," Hawk explained and gently kissed her. "You listen to me," he said, pulling Nikki into his arms, "there's a killer loose in our town, and we're going to catch whoever the killer is. I need you to be strong, though, and go into the dressing room and put on that brilliant mind of yours, okay? Go yank off the sadness I see in your eyes and put on the fighter that lives in you."

"Do I really have a choice?"

Hawk looked deep into her eyes. "Yes, you do," he said.

Staring back into Hawk's eyes, Nikki felt his words sting her heart. "Okay, Hawk...I'll go change."

"That's my girl." Hawk smiled and walked Nikki to his jeep. Before he opened the passenger side door, he reached down to his ankle and pulled up his pants leg. "Here," he said, pulling a gun out of an ankle holster.

This simple gesture seemed to say, *You have no way out, Nikki; you're trapped in the rabbit hole forever, forever, forever.* "No," Nikki said, pushing the gun away. "I have to solve this case my way, Hawk."

Instead of arguing, Hawk returned the gun to the ankle holster. "Okay," he said and drew in a deep breath, "let's go."

Nikki glanced up at the dark sky overhead and then climbed up into the passenger's seat. "Could it snow tonight?" she asked Hawk as soon as he was behind the wheel.

"Temperature is dropping pretty fast, and the rain will start in another hour or so. It's possible we could see some snow tonight. If not snow, at least some sleet."

Nikki felt a cold chill grab her heart. Suddenly, she felt like a lone character in a mystery novel, trapped in a dark night that was never going to end. "I'm ready," she told Hawk and grew very silent.

5

N ikki unlocked the front door to her chocolate shop and walked inside as if nothing were wrong. She flipped the wooden sign in the front window from "closed" to "open," removed her coat and hung it up, and walked to the back office. That's when she noticed the door to the office was ajar. "Come in, Ms. Bates," a voice called out.

Nikki felt a shiver slither down her spine, but instead of running, she drew in a deep breath and cautiously pushed the office door open. The old man was sitting in the office chair at her desk. "Who are you?" Nikki asked.

"A friend...an enemy...perhaps both," the old man said enigmatically. "Coffee, Ms. Bates?"

Nikki let her eyes look past the old man at the coffee pot sitting on her desk. "It is cold outside," she answered and stepped further into the office. "Yes, I could use some coffee."

"I believe we are going to see the first snow of the

season," the old man said. He watched Nikki retrieve a cup and fill it.

"Maybe," Nikki said and sat down on the edge of her desk. "You know who killed Mrs. Grove, right? Or am I mistaken in assuming that?"

"Oh," the old man said and picked up a white coffee cup, "assumptions are interesting little ideas full of truth and error."

"Sometimes," Nikki agreed, "but not all the time."

The old man sipped his coffee. "You've caused many problems for many people," he stated calmly. "You've challenged some very powerful men who are not apt to forget your pretty little face."

"City Hall will always be corrupt," Nikki answered. "There will always be a thorn or two that criminals stumble on."

The old man nodded very slowly as he studied Nikki's face. "Numerous people right here in this small town are very upset with you."

"I'm not out to win a popularity contest," Nikki answered and took a sip of her coffee. "You made the coffee too weak."

"I have to mind my caffeine intake," the old man explained. Continuing to study Nikki, he put down the coffee cup in his hand. "I could end your life this very second," he said.

"If you wanted me dead, I would be dead," Nikki replied bravely. "Let's just cut to the chase. You tell me who you are and what you want...or what you're after."

The old man folded his arms together. "Who I am, Ms.

Bates, is someone who can destroy your entire life with a single phone call."

"No offense," Nikki told the old man, "but I've heard all the threats before. I'm too tired to jump through the circus rings with you and play your mental games. You can tell me what you want or take a hike, okay? If you want to ruin my life, then do it. If you want to play games, play games. But do it on your own dime, because I've been fighting one criminal after another for the last few months, and I'm in no mood to chase after the crumbs you are dropping for me."

The old man grew silent. He studied Nikki with extreme caution. "There is a person in this town, Ms. Bates, whom I want. I do not know the identity of this person. It will be your duty to uncover the identity of the person I am after. If you assist me, I will tell you who killed Mrs. Grove and send you the evidence you will need to clear your name."

"And if I refuse to help?" Nikki asked.

"Your son might take a drive into a tree," the old man snapped at Nikki. "Are we clear, Ms. Bates? I can be a friend or a very deadly enemy. Do not test the limits of my patience."

"If you ever threaten my son again, I will personally dedicate my life to destroying you," Nikki snapped back and slammed down her coffee cup. "Who do you think you are? I'm not scared of you, and neither is my son. We both understand that life isn't forever, and we refuse to live scared."

"I can make you become very scared," the old man promised Nikki.

"Take your best shot." Nikki began to walk out of her office.

"Wait," the old man replied quickly. Standing up, he waved his hand. Nikki turned around. "You have guts, Ms. Bates...more guts than I expected. I'm impressed. Some of the bravest men in the world have crumbled at my threats."

"I'm not a man," Nikki told the old man. "I'm a very upset woman who wants her life back. Now you tell me who you're after, and I will help you locate this person. But so help me, if you try and play any games with me, I'll go after you the way one lion attacks another in battle."

The old man knew Nikki meant every word she said to him. "In this town," he told Nikki in a slow, low voice, "is someone who murdered my wife many, many years ago. It is time I bring justice to this person after all these years."

"I will not help you murder anyone. Deal's off," Nikki said.

"I am not talking about murdering anyone," the old man nearly hissed. "Once I locate this...hideous creature, I will send him, or her, to prison for life. You see, Ms. Bates, prison at my age is a worse fate than death."

"I see," Nikki said, struggling to read the old man's eyes. "Okay, I will help you. Meet me back here tomorrow morning at ten. Bring whatever information you have with you. Until then, I'm going home and resting. I'm going to tell Detective Hawk about our meeting. I'm not going to hide anything from him. Are we clear?"

"Ms. Bates, I can destroy your life and make you a very miserable woman. I can break your arrogant attitude at any time of my choosing. So allow me to make one thing very clear: If you fail me, your life will end in agony."

The old man walked past Nikki into the store. Nikki shook her head and closed the office door. "Take the back door out. Detective Hawk is parked outside. If he sees you—"

"Yes, yes, I know," the old man said irritably. "I'm not quite ready to leave just yet. I need to disclose a bit of information to you."

"I'm all ears," Nikki said, standing at the office door.

The old man began to explore the chocolate shop casually, the way a dog sniffs at a strange scent. "The person I am after is a killer, Ms. Bates. Your life will be in danger as you track this person for me."

"Okay," Nikki said cautiously.

"Second, whoever the killer is may know that I'm in town," the old man continued as he stopped at the front counter and examined the chocolate display case. "I suppose if the killer knows that I have arrived, he or she might try to leave."

Nikki sighed. "Please do not ask me to go chasing across the country after your killer," she said.

"I don't believe the matter will end that way," the old man confirmed. "It has been many years, and at this stage, because records show that I passed away several years ago, it's possible the killer assumes that he or she will live out the rest of their life in peace. Not so."

"You're assumed dead?" Nikki asked curiously.

"Yes, but as you can clearly see, Ms. Bates, I am very much alive and still very dangerous. Never forget that."

Nikki fought the urge to roll her eyes. "I've made a mental note of your threats," she said in a steady voice.

The old man tapped the front counter with his right index finger and began to stroll around the store. "Last, Ms. Bates," he continued, "the killer should be between the ages of forty and fifty."

"That doesn't help me," Nikki pointed out as she watched the old man circle her chocolate shop like a strange vulture searching for a certain piece of candy.

He stopped at a wooden shelf and examined a line of strawberry chocolate candy bars. "I'm aware that I am not revealing information that is helpful," he told Nikki in a low voice. "Ms. Bates, the police marked my wife's murder as unsolved and placed her case into the cold files. The killer—whoever he or she is—committed a murder and walked away like a gust of wind, leaving only a small trace of dirt behind."

"Explain," Nikki said patiently.

The old man continued to stare at the chocolate bars as a powerful gust of wind brushed up against the front door, rattling the bells hanging over the entrance. "The only pieces of evidence left at the crime scene were a few letters my wife managed to scrawl on her bedroom floor with a tube of pink lipstick. It wasn't until last year that I was able to determine their meaning."

"What happened last year?" Nikki asked.

"A computer program called 'Code Sword.' This program was created by the Department of Defense."

"The Department of Defense has programs to break codes," Nikki pointed out. "I'm assuming this Code Sword program was invented for that purpose?"

"Yes," the old man explained, "but Code Sword was created to decode an ancient Japanese language used during World War II. The American government is very interested in breaking these codes which are currently in use once more."

"Okay," Nikki said, making mental notes, "you plugged in the letters that were found written on the bedroom floor, left behind by your wife, and the program tossed the name of my town into your lap?"

"Yes," the old man replied. He raised his eyes up and focused on Nikki. "The data I retrieved from the Code Sword program gave me the name of this town."

"Why me?" Nikki asked. "And how do you know who killed Mrs. Grove?"

The old man lowered his eyes back down to the chocolate bars and took one. "May I?"

"Go ahead," Nikki said. "Now please, answer my questions."

"If you find the killer, you will find the answers you need," he informed Nikki, placing the chocolate bar into his right jacket pocket. "Ms. Bates, I have given you all the information I have. Now you must flush out the killer. The path you decide to take on your journey is your own."

"Can I at least know your wife's name?" Nikki asked, refusing to allow her voice to sound desperate.

"Jane," the old man said in a sad voice. "I will be in touch, Ms. Bates."

Nikki watched him leave through the back door and vanish. "Great," she sighed miserably. "I've got to locate a gust of wind and find out who murdered Mrs. Grove...Happy autumn, Nikki."

Standing silently next to the front counter, Nikki listened to the strong winds howling outside. The winds seemed to be changing the world into a mysterious, dangerous whisper that would soon shatter into screams. She began to feel lost, isolated and strange. "All I need is a fedora, a long overcoat, a dusty office, and for everything to go black and white," she whispered.

She heard the front door open and saw Hawk appear. "Pop called," he told her in a regretful voice. "We better get back to the station. A bunch of locals are arriving with their pitchforks and torches."

"The old man was in here," Nikki told Hawk.

"What?!" Hawk exclaimed. "When? Where did he go? Are you okay?"

Nikki raised her hand. "Slow down, big guy," she begged. "Yes, I'm fine. But I've got my work cut out for me. Hawk, now I have to find two killers instead of one."

Hawk listened as Nikki revealed to him every word the old man had spoken to her. Rubbing his chin, he walked to the shelf holding the strawberry chocolate bars. "He took a candy bar?"

Nikki nodded. "I know I shouldn't have let him take the candy, Hawk, but what choice did I have? I'm sure that old scarecrow had a gun hidden on his body."

"You did the right thing."

"What do you make of all this?" Nikki asked, walking up to Hawk and placing her head on his shoulder.

Hawk gently patted the side of Nikki's face with a warm, caring hand. "I'm not sure, but I'm going to try and find out. Come on, we better get back down to the station."

Nikki locked up her store and drove back to the police station with Hawk. Sitting silently in the passenger seat, she watched the wind toss the leaves across streets and past cozy homes and buildings. But instead of feeling warm and secure in her small town, Nikki felt very afraid. When Hawk pulled his jeep into the parking lot at the police station, and she saw a crowd of angry people yelling at Chief Daily, she closed her eyes. "Oh, Hawk..."

Hawk patted her shoulder. "Hey, now, you listen to me. You're a fighter. Don't you pay any mind to what these loud-mouths are screaming."

The crowd of angry people were yelling "Killer!" and "Murderer!" at Chief Daily, who was struggling to quiet them. Standing in front of the main entrance, he raised his hands into the cold air. "Everyone, listen to me—Ms. Bates is innocent until proven guilty in a court of law. Now, you have every right to gather and protest...peacefully. Right now, you're disturbing the peace."

"Nikki Bates is a curse!" a woman in her mid-fifties yelled at Chief Daily.

"Why are you protecting a killer?" a man hollered. "When voting season arrives, we'll vote in a man who will protect the people instead of a killer!"

"Nikki Bates poisoned poor Mrs. Grove," a second woman yelled. "That awful woman has brought nothing but darkness to our town!"

Chief Daily narrowed his eyes and toughened his voice. "Now you listen to me. I am still the Chief of Police in this town. If you want to vote in a new Chief of Police when voting season arrives, do so. But for now, I'm the law, and I will not tolerate anyone—and I mean anyone—

slandering another person. If Ms. Bates is guilty, she will answer for her crime. If she is innocent, I expect everyone standing here to leave her alone and keep your mouths shut!"

The crowd of people stared at Chief Daily in shock. Never before had any one of them heard the man speak in such a harsh way. Expecting to bully a man who appeared to be a weak civil servant, they quickly learned that Chief Daily could become a fierce grizzly bear when pushed into a corner. One man, however, was undeterred. "Get rid of that woman!" he yelled at Chief Daily, "or someone else just might."

The man didn't see Hawk walk up behind him. Hawk grabbed the man, slung him down onto the sidewalk, and handcuffed him. "I don't like threats being made in my town," he growled.

"You're...hurting me!" the man began to cry like the coward he was.

Hawk snatched the man to his feet and shoved him toward Chief Daily. "The rest of you take a hike," he ordered the crowd.

"We have a right to be here," a woman in her late sixties informed Hawk in an aggrieved voice.

Hawk glanced back toward his jeep and then at the crowd. "Do you people really believe Nikki Bates poisoned Mrs. Grove? Come on, folks," he said in a way that told the crowd they were acting like silly children. "Nikki Bates is an intelligent woman. If she wanted to kill anyone, trust me, she would carry off the crime so brilliantly that no one would ever be able to convict her.

Why would she poison a woman with her own chocolate?"

"Everyone knows you and that...*woman*...are an item, now, Detective," the older woman snapped sourly at Hawk. "Perhaps it's time to request that you resign your position and relocate."

Hawk grinned. "Lady, Ms. Bates and I are going to grow old in this town. We're not going anywhere."

Nikki drew in a deep breath, got out of the jeep, and walked up next to Hawk. She studied the crowd with sad eyes. "I'm going to find the person who killed Mrs. Grove," she promised. "But I need to make one fact very clear: I'm not going to find the killer to please anyone standing here. You see, the killer has murdered an innocent woman in an attempt to destroy my life. Now, I don't know how people in the north handle threats, but I don't take them lightly. I'm a fighter, and I intend to fight. If any of you don't like me living here and wish for me to leave, well, get over it, because I'm not going anywhere. This is my home now."

"You don't belong here," a woman screamed at Nikki. "You're a curse!"

"No," Nikki replied calmly, "I'm not a curse, Mrs. Hetherington. I'm a woman who wishes to settle down and live a peaceful life. Right now, there is a killer loose in this town who wants to destroy my life. I intend to fight. Now, you can all hate me and yell poisonous words in my face, but rest assured, I've dealt with worse than you."

"Are you threatening us?" the handcuffed man hissed at Nikki.

"I'm simply pointing out that I will not be run out of

town," Nikki replied in a stable, stern tone. "If you people want a fight, I'll go twelve rounds with each and every one of you. I will not be bullied, and I will not tolerate anyone bullying the people I love and care about."

Chief Daily smiled at Hawk. Nikki was holding her ground against the worst the town had to offer—against people who were cold-hearted and believed the world revolved around their views and beliefs. Now those same people were challenging a momma lion who wasn't in the mood to deal with a bunch of whiny, weak mice that had nothing else better to do than chew holes in the cloth of truth, justice, and integrity. "Protest on the sidewalk across the street," Chief Daily informed the crowd.

Nikki held her ground. She locked eyes with them. The faces in the crowd stared back at her with hatred, but slowly, one by one, each person in the crowd walked away and went home. "I'll go book this guy," Chief Daily told Hawk and pulled the handcuffed man inside.

"I'll sue you for every penny!" the man yelled.

"You can call your lawyer after I book you for criminal threatening," Chief Daily told the man.

Nikki looked at Hawk. "I made some fresh enemies," she said miserably.

Hawk looked down into Nikki's upset eyes. He rubbed the back of his neck and then looked around. "You know, Nikki, this town, like every town dotted across the map, is filled with the good and the bad. You have to have faith in the good, though. I counted ten people in that bunch, Nikki. Now, if a hundred people had shown up, I might be worried. So what if ten whiny adults showed up here at the station to act like children? You backed them down,

36

and they'll continue to back down because that's the kind of people they are...cowards."

"Maybe so," Nikki agreed, "but the person who killed Mrs. Grove is deadly. Who knows, Hawk? The killer could have been anyone in that crowd of people."

"Maybe," Hawk agreed, raising his eyes toward the gray sky overhead. "I'm going to sleep at your cabin tonight, okay? Your couch is pretty comfortable."

Nikki hugged Hawk's arm. "I was hoping you would," she admitted. Biting down on her lower lip, she stood silently and then spoke: "The old man said that the woman who was murdered was named Jane. Hawk, I need you to do some digging and find out who this woman is. Maybe then I will be able to shed some light on the old man's identity."

"Needle in a haystack," Hawk replied. "I'll make you a deal. Tonight, I'll cook dinner at your cabin, and while you're making coffee and dessert, I'll make some calls."

"Sounds good. Tomorrow I'll need to start searching for the killers, but tonight I need to gather my thoughts together and make a plan of attack. I wish I could just go home and make some homemade cocoa and some peppermint chocolate, cuddle up with a good book, read, and fall asleep in my pajamas."

Hawk wrapped his arm around Nikki's shoulder. "Let's get inside. The temperature is dropping, and the wind is getting rough."

Nikki allowed Hawk to walk her inside the police station. Her little town was now a dangerous, dark alley with deadly claws lurking in its shadows.

6

"Well?" Lidia asked Hawk impatiently.

Hawk sat down at the kitchen table. For a few seconds, he listened to the screaming winds throwing sleet against the cabin. "I was on the phone a long time," he finally said.

Nikki brought Hawk a fresh cup of hot coffee. "Was your friend able to help?"

Hawk looked across the table at Lidia and Tori and then up at Nikki. "Yes, she and her husband lived in Atlanta. They were there when you lived there, Nikki. Her name was Jane...Bates," Hawk told Nikki.

"Bates?" Nikki asked in a whisper. "Really?"

Lidia stood up, walked over to Nikki, and pushed her bangs away from her eyes. "Honey?" she asked.

Nikki glanced up into Lidia's face. "A possible member of my family could have been murdered," Nikki said in a strained voice.

"The last name is probably a mistake," Tori insisted.

Hawk shook his head. "My friend searched every cold

case file with the name 'Jane' attached to it. The name alone wasn't much help."

"The lipstick letters," Nikki said.

Hawk nodded. "The lettering found scrawled on the bedroom floor was the ticket."

"What is the name of the deceased woman's husband?" Nikki asked.

"Oliver Bates. He went missing last year while hiking in Chile. His body was never found," Hawk explained.

"Last year was when the old man—I mean, Oliver Bates—came into contact with the Code Sword program," Nikki told everyone. Refusing to sit like a crippled child, she forced strength back into her legs and stood up. "Hawk, what is the last known address of Oliver Bates?"

"191 Greenview Drive, Atlanta, Georgia," Hawk said and waited for her response.

Nikki nodded. "And what was the address where the murder took place?" she asked.

"Same address," Hawk informed Nikki. "191 Greenview Drive is the address of an old plantation-style home. The place is now being used as an art museum."

"Did Oliver Bates sell the house before he faked his death?" Nikki asked. Walking to the kitchen counter, she picked up a cup of hot chocolate and took a sip. Lidia and Tori watched Nikki transform into a sharp, alert, confident detective, yet Lidia also noticed a deep, strange fear hidden in Nikki's beautiful eyes.

"Yep," Hawk replied and sat back down. Picking up his coffee cup, he took a sip. "The man also cashed out his stocks and other investments. All in all, he walked away with enough money to live the rest of his life in luxury."

Nikki bit down on her lower lip. Oliver Bates isn't planning to remain in America, she told herself. Looking at Hawk, she studied his eyes. "The last name and location could be a coincidence," she said.

"It could be. The name Bates isn't that uncommon, after all."

"Right," Nikki agreed. Studying the cup of hot chocolate in her hands, she closed her eyes and listened to the howling winds. A powerful cold front from Canada was pushing into Vermont with icy fingers. The ten-day weather outlook had been changed. Instead of cool autumn temperatures with clear skies, the weather was now calling for icy temperatures filled with sleet and freezing rain that would eventually change into snow. Hearing the sleet hitting the kitchen window, Nikki shivered. "I don't know what's happening," she whispered, "but I'm going to find out."

Hawk watched Nikki leave the kitchen. Lidia and Tori shook their heads at Hawk when he began to follow her. "Let Nikki be alone," Lidia told Hawk in a kind voice. Sitting down, she picked up her cup of coffee and took a sip. "This Oliver person, he's connected to Nikki somehow?"

Tori cast her worried eyes at Hawk. "Please, the truth," she pleaded.

Hawk looked at his coffee. "It's possible," he explained in a careful voice. "The last name, the location, the man showing up at the chocolate shop... It's an awful lot of coincidence."

Lidia looked at Tori and then back at Hawk. "How bad is this situation, Hawk?"

"Oliver Bates is forcing Nikki to locate the person who murdered his wife. He claims if Nikki accomplishes her task, he will tell her who murdered Mrs. Grove and even send her enough evidence to seal the case." Hawk scratched his chin. "But my gut is telling me that maybe the person who murdered Mrs. Grove just might be the same person who killed Oliver Bates' wife."

"How is that possible?" Tori asked, confused.

Hawk picked up his coffee cup. "I've been kicking the ball around some, and I think that the killer knows Oliver Bates is onto him...or her. The killer could also know that Oliver Bates might try and contact Nikki for help. So what does he—or she—do? Attack Nikki and try to have her arrested for murder."

"If Nikki is out of the picture, then she can't track down the killer," Tori said.

Hawk nodded. "Young lady, someday you could make a good detective."

Lidia rested her chin on her right palm. "How is Nikki connected to Oliver Bates, though? Yes, the last name and location are striking, but there has to be more, Hawk."

"Yep," Hawk agreed, "and that's where I'm running into a wall. Guys, I don't know all of Nikki's past. But it's clear Nikki doesn't know Oliver Bates or his wife. Or so it seems. Right now, we need Nikki to piece some of the puzzle together for us. Until she can, all we can do is sit tight."

"How long will it be before the crime lab sends you the report on the chocolate?" Lidia asked Hawk. "The report should be very helpful."

"Tomorrow," Hawk answered Lidia. "After Nikki and I

came back to the station, Pop grabbed the chocolate and headed downstate to the crime lab himself. He'll be back tomorrow with the results."

"I'm worried about this Oliver Bates taking a candy bar from the store," Lidia told Hawk. "He might try and frame Nikki for another murder."

"I've thought about that," Hawk replied, equally worried.

Tori looked past Hawk toward the kitchen window. She thought about Nikki's eyes. "Nikki is so sad."

"All she wants is peace," Lidia said. "That woman seems to be a magnet for trouble, though."

Hawk looked down at his cup of coffee. "I know," he sighed. "I just pray this is her last case. I was kinda hoping we would have a nice, quiet winter filled with warm fires and long walks in the snow. After my wife and I divorced, I swore I wouldn't get serious about another woman. But Nikki, she sure is different. She knocked my socks off!" Hawk laughed and blushed. "I don't know what the woman sees in an old jerk like me. I...it's nice to care about someone and have them care about you."

Lidia reached over and patted Hawk's hand. "Nikki does care about you, Hawk. We all do."

"And you and Nikki are so good together," Tori told Hawk. "I'm happy she has someone like you to care about her."

Hawk closed his eyes and rubbed his nose. "If I really cared about Nikki, I would take her and leave this town."

"No!" Lidia begged.

"There's nothing wrong with our town," Tori insisted. "Some of the people are rotten apples, but not everyone.

Nikki loves her new life in Vermont, Hawk. I doubt she would run away."

"I know. That's the problem. Even if I wanted to run away with Nikki, she would refuse. Nikki is a fighter. Me...I feel like I'm getting older and older before my time. I came to this town to investigate unpaid traffic tickets, not murder. I left New York to get away from that life."

Lidia patted Hawk's hand again. "The Lord has His reasons. Let me get you a refill on coffee."

"Thanks."

An hour later, Nikki walked back into the kitchen. She saw Hawk, Lidia and Tori sitting at the table, talking and eating a slice of coconut cake apiece. "Jane Bates was my great aunt," she said in a calm voice. "I've been online, studying my genealogy. Oliver Bates was my dad's adopted brother. No one in my family ever told me about him."

"Okay, we have a connection," Hawk clapped his hands together.

Nikki put the empty coffee cup in her hand down into the kitchen sink. "Hawk, we have a connection but more riddles than I can handle tonight. I'm fighting a lot of confusion and fatigue. I guess...what I'm really wondering is how Jane Bates managed to write the name of this town on her bedroom floor with lipstick...and why did I choose this town to call home?"

"It's getting late. Maybe we should all try and get some sleep," Lidia suggested.

Nikki leaned against the kitchen sink. "This weather is going to be difficult," she said and looked at the back door.

"Nikki, dear, did you hear what I said?" Lidia asked worriedly. "Maybe we should all try and get some rest."

"Huh? Oh, uh, sure," Nikki said. Feeling lost in a thick fog, she shook her head and forced a smile to her lips. "I'm sorry...I guess I'm a little scatterbrained tonight."

Hawk studied Nikki's face. He was worried. "We're all going to stand watch in three-hour shifts tonight," he explained. "I'm taking the first shift. Tori, you'll take the second shift. Nikki, you can grab the third, and Lidia will finish the fourth."

"Why?" Lidia asked. "Do you believe someone might try and break into the cabin?"

Hawk bit down on his lower lip. "It's dark and freezing outside. This is the kind of night killers love to work in. We need to all be alert."

Nikki closed her eyes and imagined outside. In the icy darkness, she saw two hideous eyes staring at her cabin. *Nikki...Nikki Bates...I'm coming for you...coming for you...coming for you...* Nikki flung her eyes open. "I think I'll go soak in a hot bath for a while and then get some sleep. Tori, wake me for my shift, honey, okay? 'Night, everyone."

Nikki hurried out of the kitchen and into her bedroom. Closing the bedroom door behind her she clasped her nervous hands together. "I was brought to this town for a reason..." she whispered and then ran into her bathroom and slammed the door tightly shut.

Nikki was shocked when she woke up and saw morning light coming through her bedroom window. Alarmed, she grabbed a pink, fluffy robe, threw it on, and ran out into the living room. Finding the living room empty, she rushed into the kitchen. Hawk was sitting at the table, eating a sandwich and drinking coffee. "Why didn't anyone wake me?" she asked.

Hawk yawned. "Blame Tori. She didn't wake anyone. She pulled your shift and Lidia's shift. I put her to bed about twenty minutes ago. Breakfast?"

Nikki looked out the kitchen window. The winds were screaming viciously. She shivered. "I'll have some coffee. Forgive my appearance."

Hawk found Nikki's messy hair and sleepy face beautiful. "You look like a princess."

Nikki examined her messy hair with her hands. "No makeup, messy hair...I look awful."

Hawk stood up, walked over to Nikki, and kissed her

before she could run away. "You look beautiful," he insisted. "Now sit down. I'll pour you a cup of coffee."

Nikki smiled and sat down. She looked at Hawk's sandwich and smiled again. "A bachelor's breakfast, huh?"

"Turkey, cheese, tomato, all sprinkled with cayenne pepper," he told Nikki, pouring her a cup of coffee. "Cayenne is good for the heart and wakes up the taste buds."

"I see," Nikki said and wondered how anyone could put cayenne pepper on a sandwich so early in the morning.

Hawk set Nikki's cup of coffee on the kitchen table and sat down. "Ice is sticking to the trees and the roads. Power is out in certain areas. I'm surprised we still have power here. As you can hear, the wind outside has settled in pretty good. It's going to be a rough day, Nikki. I called Pop. He's stuck downstate. Our best bet is to chance getting back to the station and sitting still for a while."

Nikki picked up her coffee cup and took a careful sip. "One step at a time, Hawk. Has Chief Daily received the results from the crime lab?"

Hawk nodded. "He didn't let the crime lab close until he got the results."

"And?"

"Years back," Hawk told Nikki in a cop tone, "the military experimented with chemicals that would induce an immediate coma. The idea was to spray the substance on the battlefield, paralyze the enemy, and save lives...or so the reports on the darn stuff states. But this chemical, C5T-91, did more than put someone into a coma. It lowered the heart rate to the point the heart could no longer function."

"Research grants were canceled, and the chemical was transported to a high-security warehouse and stored, right?" Nikki asked.

"That's the official story."

"The storage location of this chemical is right here in Vermont, right?"

"A few miles away from the Center for Disease Control," Hawk confirmed.

"So how did our killer get this chemical?" Nikki asked herself rather than Hawk.

"Nikki, Oliver Bates may be playing a game of some sort with you," Hawk answered in a worried voice. "No one can just waltz right into a secure warehouse and walk out with a deadly chemical."

"But someone—the killer—obviously did," Nikki said, and then a theory struck her. "Hawk, what if Oliver Bates killed Mrs. Grove in an attempt to blackmail me? He did say he would send me evidence."

"Evidence that could be altered to match a need," Hawk confirmed.

Nikki took a sip of her coffee. "It's possible. We need to find out who Oliver Bates worked for."

"I'll find out today," Hawk promised Nikki. Looking into her face, he noticed a peculiar expression. It was as if Nikki were lost inside her own mind. "Are you okay?"

Nikki put down her coffee cup. She began to speak but then paused. Closing her eyes, she struggled to clear her mind. "Hawk, ever since yesterday, I feel like I'm lost in this thick fog. I feel like I'm trapped inside myself, searching for the answer to a very dark secret. I can't explain what I'm feeling..."

"Try," Hawk gently urged her.

Nikki kept her eyes closed. Listening to the howling winds outside, she fought to place her confused thoughts into words that would somehow make sense. "Hawk, why did I choose Maple Hills as my new home? Or maybe I should ask: *How* did I choose Maple Hills as my new home?"

"What do you mean?"

Nikki slowly opened her eyes, against her will, as if they were being pulled open by a cruel prison guard. "When I decided to leave Atlanta, I didn't choose Vermont as my new home. I chose a little town in North Carolina that was snuggled up against the Smoky Mountains. Yet somehow, I ended up in Maple Hills. How?"

Hawk shook his head. "You tell me."

"I can't," Nikki said in a frustrated voice. She walked away from the kitchen counter and began pacing around the kitchen. "Up until yesterday, I never even questioned how I arrived in Maple Hills. My conscious mind just assumed that I had somehow made the decision to relocate here, but after my meeting with Oliver Bates at my store...I don't know, Hawk. It's like a crack formed in my subconscious mind, and these ugly, dark secrets are leaking out like invisible ink...and I'm trying to see what the ink is writing on my mind. Does any of this make sense?"

Hawk watched Nikki as she stopped walking and looked out the kitchen window into the dark, stormy morning. "No," he answered honestly. "Nikki, you're the one who has to make sense of what is going on inside your mind. When you do, we'll solve this case."

Nikki thumped the kitchen counter with her fist. "Hawk, why did I come to Maple Hills? Who brought me here?"

"What?" Hawk asked.

She turned and faced him. "Huh?"

"What did you say?" Hawk asked.

"Why did I come to Maple Hills?"

"No," Hawk said carefully, "after that."

"I..." Nikki began to speak and then stopped. Her eyes grew wide. "Who brought me to Maple Hills?" she whispered as a horrible, deep chill grabbed her heart. Closing her eyes, she saw a shiny object swinging before her eyes. "Who brought me to Maple Hills?" she whispered again.

The telephone hanging on the wall next to the refrigerator rang. Startled, Nikki threw her eyes open. Hawk was staring at her but didn't say a word. "I better answer the call," she said.

"Okay."

Nikki picked up the phone. "Hello?"

"Horrible weather we're having, isn't it, Ms. Bates?" Oliver Bates greeted Nikki in a low voice.

"Could be worse," Nikki said and pointed at the phone. "It's him," she mouthed to Hawk.

Hawk got to his feet, hurried over to Nikki and pushed his ear close to the phone. "Tell Detective Daily to sit back down," Oliver told Nikki in a stern voice.

Hawk looked at Nikki and then threw his eyes around the kitchen. Without saying a word, he moved away from the phone and sat back down. "Okay, he sat back down," Nikki told Oliver as anger erupted in her heart. "You broke into my cabin, didn't you?" she demanded.

"I'm a very cautious man," Oliver explained to Nikki, "but to answer your question, no, I did not trespass and violate your privacy. I have many resources at my disposal, Ms. Bates. Satellites, floating far above our heads, allow one to have eyes in numerous places."

Some distance away, in a pleasant, comfortable rental house, Oliver sat at a wooden kitchen table looking at the screen of a large laptop. And there on the screen was Nikki Bates standing in her kitchen, wearing her pink robe. Picking up a brown mug, he patiently took a sip of hot honey water with just a dash of lemon. As he took a sip of it, he watched Nikki glance over her shoulder toward Hawk and then focus on the kitchen wall. "Talk," she finally said.

Oliver set down the mug. He felt cunning and brilliant —dangerous and daring. Dressed in a gray suit that always made him feel empowered, Oliver calmly clasped his hands together and stared at Nikki on the screen. The woman was obviously very sharp, yet she was no match for his mind. "Detective Hawk made a few interesting phone calls last night, did he not?"

"Stop it," Nikki snapped. "We know your name is Oliver Bates, okay?"

Hawk watched Nikki slowly begin to fall apart at the seams. Some hideous enemy hidden inside her mind was tormenting her, crippling her ability to remain in control of her emotions and thoughts. "Get it together," Hawk told Nikki in a stern voice.

Nikki turned and looked at him. "I'm trying," she whispered desperately. Tears slowly began falling from her scared eyes. "What did you do to me?" she begged Oliver.

"I told you that I could destroy you," Oliver informed Nikki. "Now that I have your full attention, perhaps you will do as you're told. You were assigned a task. You must find a killer. Are we clear?"

"We're clear, yes," Nikki said and wiped at her tears. "I will do whatever is needed to find the person who killed your wife."

"We are family, Ms. Bates, are we not? And shouldn't one family member tend to the needs of another family member?"

"You're not my family," Nikki told Oliver, disgusted. "You're a monster."

"Now, now, was that very nice?" he asked. "Watch your words with me, Ms. Bates, or I will be forced to punish you."

"I don't know what is happening," Nikki said, "but since our meeting yesterday, I feel as if some hidden door in my mind is slowly opening up. I became aware of that feeling when I returned home last night. But when I found out you were the adopted brother of my daddy, the feeling intensified. Whatever game you're playing, after I find the person who killed your wife, I'm going to end your game."

"Such rudeness!" Oliver snapped. "But for now, I will ignore your hateful gestures. Today, Ms. Bates, you have work to do. Get out and begin your search. If you refuse, I will make sure your son is the one punished for your refusal to work instead of you."

Nikki closed her eyes. The image of a sweet, warm,

newborn baby smiling up into her face graced her mind. "Leave my son out of your sick game," Nikki warned Oliver. "If you touch him, I'll go after you with every resource I have."

"Do not threaten me," Oliver hissed.

"You need me," Nikki snapped. "If you didn't need me, you would have chosen someone else to track down the person who killed your wife. You have faked your death, sold your stocks and investments, and now you're hiding out in Maple Hills hoping I will find the person who killed your wife. Why, Oliver? You're obviously a man with many talents; why do you need me? Why not hire a slew of private investigators to track down the killer?"

Oliver gritted his teeth. "Get to work, Ms. Bates, or your son—"

"My son isn't a coward, and neither am I," Nikki stated, "but let me make this promise to you, Oliver Bates: If you touch my son, it will be you that I go after. I will send your information onto every social media platform known to mankind. I will write story after story about you. I will go to every news and media outlet there is and make your name viral. And since the governor of Vermont has personally stated that he is indebted to me for my services, I will ask him to repay his debt by supporting me in my quest to destroy you. And before you reply, let me also remind you that a person who fakes his own death isn't someone the government is pleased with. No, you faked your own death because whoever you were working for decided it was time to dispose of you, isn't that right, Oliver?"

"That's my girl," Hawk whispered proudly.

Oliver kept his hands clasped together. Feeling anger boil up into his chest, he nearly exploded in rage. Instead, he drew in five deep breaths and forced self-control over his words. "Tick-tock, Ms. Bates. The sand is draining. Find the killer. I will be in touch."

Nikki slammed the phone down and wiped at her tears. "No more tears," she said in a desperate voice. "I've got work to do."

Hawk stood up and walked over to Nikki. Gently, he pulled her into his arms. "It's going to be okay," he promised.

"Is it?" Closing her eyes, Nikki saw the shiny object swinging back and forth before her eyes. "Oh Hawk, what did that awful man do to me? Why was I brought to Maple Hills?"

Hawk knew every word he or Nikki spoke would reach the ears of Oliver Bates. "Get dressed," he told Nikki in a low whisper. "We have work to do."

"Work?" Nikki almost laughed to herself. "Hawk, are you serious? How am I supposed to find the person who killed Jane Bates? Look outside. No one will be in town today. I guess the diner might be open, but that's all."

Something in Nikki's voice struck Hawk as odd. Looking deep into her eyes, Hawk quickly caught a glimpse that only he could understand. "You have to try," he told her. "Go get dressed, huh?"

Nikki left the kitchen, looking like a woman who was severely confused and beaten down. She walked to her bedroom, threw on a thick, gray sweater dress, dark green winter leggings, a pair of brown walking boots and a gray ski cap. When she returned to the kitchen, Lidia and Tori were waiting. "Where are you going?" Lidia asked, concerned.

Nikki forced a smile to her lips. Lidia was still dressed in a pair of pink pajamas, and Tori was wrapped in a blue robe that dropped down to a pair of fuzzy bunny slippers. "I have work to do," she explained.

Lidia didn't fall for Nikki's smile. "We're getting dressed."

"Good idea," Hawk agreed. "You and Tori need to relocate yourselves to the police station today. Remember, you're both still under investigation."

Tori looked at Hawk. With his eyes, he told her to listen and not speak. Lidia immediately understood Hawk's expression. "Okay, okay, already—don't remind us," she fussed and grabbed Tori's hand. "Come on, dear, let's go get dressed."

Nikki walked to the coffee pot and unplugged it. "I was thinking," she said without disguising her voice, "that if the person who killed Jane Bates is in Maple Hills, then a good place to start will be the courthouse. I need to check the public records."

"For what?" Hawk asked curiously.

"I'm not sure yet," Nikki confessed and rubbed the back of her neck. "Hawk, drop me off at the courthouse on the way to the police station, okay? I'll be a while. In the meantime, you can continue investigating the murder of Mrs. Grove."

"Are you sure?" Hawk asked.

Nikki tossed a quick wink at Hawk. "I'm sure. It's always safe to be in a public facility on a day like this...on a day that a killer prefers."

"Sure thing," Hawk said, even though the idea of leaving Nikki alone at the courthouse didn't sit well with him. Picking up his cup, he drained the rest of the coffee and aimed his eyes toward the living room. "I'll go warm up the jeep. You hurry those ladies up for me, okay?"

"I will," Nikki said. As soon as Hawk walked out of the kitchen, she closed her eyes. "I'm...beginning...to remember..." she whispered as the bright, shiny object swung back and forth in front of her eyes.

8

An hour later, Nikki walked into a warm, single-story building that smelled of pine and cinnamon. Shaking sleet off her thick, green, wool coat, she hurried up to a glass window, walking across a beautiful brown carpet in her wet boots. A young woman in her late twenties spotted Nikki approaching and put down a magazine. "Can I help you?" she asked.

Nikki continued to shake the sleet off her coat and spoke in a polite, calm tone. "I need to access your public records, please."

The young woman stared at Nikki coldly. Aware of who was asking to see the public records, she debated with herself whether to deny the request or allow it. Of course, if she denied Nikki access to the public records, she would be violating the law and might, as a result, risk being canned from her job. She brushed a piece of lint off the blue sweater she was wearing and then checked her short brown hair. "My mother doesn't like you," she told Nikki.

Nikki ignored the insult and signed her name on a guest registry form attached to a brown clipboard sitting on the counter under the window. "Which way to the public records room?"

"No one likes you," the young woman continued in a hateful voice.

"I wasn't that popular in high school either, sweetie," Nikki replied in a sharp voice. "Now, either you tell me which way to the public records room, or I ask to see your supervisor. You are a public servant. Your job is to assist the public, not harass them. The cell phone in my purse has been recording our conversation. Shall I ask your supervisor to take a listen?"

The young woman glanced at the white purse Nikki had set down on the counter. "Through the main door, fourth door down on the right," she said. "I'm sorry. I didn't mean—"

"Save it for the courts," Nikki said coldly and grabbed her purse.

"Have a nice day," the young woman called out, hoping to sound authentic. Nikki rolled her eyes and hurried to the heavy wooden door and pulled it open. She stepped through it and walked down a long hallway lined with doors. When she saw Oliver Bates standing in front of the door leading into the public records room, she paused. *Be strong*, she told herself.

Oliver waved at Nikki. "Nice to see you again, Ms. Bates," he called out.

Nikki approached him cautiously. "I have work to do," she said angrily. "I don't need you micro-managing my every move."

"I intend to watch," Oliver warned her in a stern tone. "I don't need you to withhold any new findings you might...accidentally...discover."

"Fine," Nikki said and pushed past him. Stepping into the public records room, she was disappointed to find that the room had no windows. Instead, it was cramped, lined with old metal filing cabinets and a single, wooden table on a dark brown tile floor. Oliver stepped in behind Nikki and closed the door. "Don't get in my way," Nikki said and placed her purse down onto the table.

"Surely not." Oliver smiled hideously.

Nikki carefully watched Oliver remove his gray coat and then a gray fedora. Methodically, he placed his coat onto the back of a wooden chair and then neatly put his hat down onto the table, next to Nikki's purse. "Such horrible weather to walk an animal in, isn't it, Ms. Bates?" he asked. "This morning I learned that my poor dog isn't fond of this weather, poor thing."

"I wouldn't know. I don't have any pets," Nikki replied. Hesitantly, she turned her back to Oliver and studied metal filing cabinets. "What year would you say the killer arrived in Maple Hills?" she asked.

"That's for you to discover," Oliver replied. Sitting down, he patiently watched Nikki approach the filing cabinets. "And what are we looking for in particular?"

"If you want me to find the person who killed your wife I will need all the assistance you can offer. What year would you say the killer arrived in Maple Hills?" Nikki asked again.

"I can't answer your question because I do not know," Oliver explained.

"Fine," Nikki said as her eyes roamed from one filing cabinet to another. "Mr. Bates, you have been watching my home, so you must know by now I am aware of the chemical inserted into the chocolate that killed Mrs. Grove."

"Yes," Oliver said in a steady voice, "I am aware. This is to be expected, though. Why do you ask?"

Nikki turned and faced Oliver. "It's possible you are playing a game with me. Perhaps you even killed Mrs. Grove to frame me, to coerce me to find your wife's killer."

"The games we play are always composed of uncertainties, now aren't they?" Oliver said as he narrowed his eyes. "The outcome will become clear when you find Jane's killer. Now get to work."

Nikki removed her coat and plunged into the filing cabinets with skilled hands and a sharp, focused mind. But slowly she grew distracted as her mind kept grabbing at the image of the shining object, swinging back and forth in front of her eyes. Sitting down at the table across from Oliver, she put down a brown file. "My daddy never mentioned you to me," she said casually.

Oliver watched Nikki open the file and begin investigating the contents. "I was, as they say, the black sheep of the family, Ms. Bates. Your grandparents adopted me, this is true. But it wasn't long before they also deserted me."

Nikki sensed bitterness in Oliver's voice. "Why?" she asked, reading a tax record belonging to a man named Ronald Botterman.

Oliver's eyes flashed with anger. "Why?" he asked,

allowing his voice to ring with the anger that was welling up in his chest. "Why?"

"Yes, why?" Nikki asked again.

"Because your father was the perfect one, and I, Ms. Bates, was the horrible creature who needed to be hidden beneath the bed. I could never please my adoptive parents, no matter how many attempts I made to do so. Your father was a miserable child and a filthy young man. He smoked, stole, and committed crimes. Did he ever suffer the consequences? No. But if I so much as forgot to make my bed, I would face certain beatings with words and hands."

"My daddy was a wonderful man," Nikki objected. "You make him sound as if he were a monster."

"Wasn't he?" Oliver hissed.

Nikki shrugged. "We're all a little mischievous when we're young. I remember taking a candy bar from a store when I was ten years old because a friend dared me to. That doesn't make me a monster."

"That makes you a thief, Ms. Bates. We must not romanticize our crimes."

"Sure, I was a thief," Nikki agreed, "but I was also very young and silly. We grow out of those childish stages in life, though."

Oliver stared at Nikki with hateful eyes. The woman had simply, with very little effort, swatted away his powerful convictions about his stepbrother. "Why are you looking into this man's records?" he asked, determined to remain in control.

"Ronald Botterman moved to Maple Hills soon after your wife was found murdered," Nikki explained, examining the records. "I'm trying to compile a list of people who moved to Maple Hills in the time frame your wife was murdered. Is that okay with you?"

"Very well," Oliver said, granting Nikki permission to move forward. "But I do not see pen or pad?"

"I make mental notes," Nikki assured him. "I never forget a single detail."

"Really?" Oliver asked and then grinned. "I might say that is vain, Ms. Bates."

Nikki closed the file. "Nah," she said and stood up, "I'm pretty good at remembering stuff...except where I put my car keys."

Oliver watched Nikki walk back to the filing cabinet from which she had removed the file. "You are a lovely woman. It's such a pity that your husband filed for divorce."

"It happens," Nikki replied, feeling a sharp dagger dig into her heart.

"Does it?" Oliver asked. "Yes, I suppose it does."

Nikki removed another file and walked back to the table. Sitting down, she quickly glanced into Oliver's soulless eyes. "It's difficult for me to believe that a man like you could love a woman," she said in a curious voice. "Your wife must have been some woman to put up with the likes of you."

Oliver grinned at Nikki's insult instead of becoming enraged. "Jane was a terrific woman. She never tolerated my...foul habits."

"I bet," Nikki said. "Is that why she ended up dead?"

Oliver quit grinning. "Pardon me?" he asked as his face went flat and cold.

Nikki looked across the table at Oliver. "I'm just implying that she might have crossed someone, you know? It's obvious she had an enemy, Oliver. It doesn't take a rocket scientist to figure that much out."

"Oh...yes, of course," Oliver said and forced his mind to calm down. "But I haven't the slightest idea who could have wanted Jane dead."

"Maybe it wasn't Jane the killer was after," Nikki suggested. "Have you ever considered the killer was after you? Let's face it, you didn't sell off your stocks and investments and fake your own death because you were popular at work."

"I do not appreciate your accusations, Ms. Bates. Remember, I control you."

Nikki slammed the file in her hands closed. "And with a few clicks of a mouse, every social media outlet in the world will control you," she fired back. "Let's get this straight, okay? I'll find your wife's killer, and then you take a hike out of town after you provide me with the evidence you promised."

Oliver narrowed his eyes and stared at Nikki with vicious hatred, yet he decided not to walk into a battle of words with the woman. Nikki's punishment would come at the end, he reminded himself. "I have considered that I was the killer's target instead of my wife, Ms. Bates. That does not mitigate my responsibility to track down the person who committed the crime."

"Okay," Nikki said and unclenched her mental fist, "fair enough. Today I'll make a list of possible suspects and then go home and research each person online. I should have a few leads by tomorrow."

Oliver leaned back in his chair and folded his arms over his chest. "I do not like your detective friend. I want him to stay away from you while you are employed in my services."

"No way," Nikki objected, "Hawk and I are a team. Hawk stays at my side."

"Detective Daily is such an...ignorant man," Oliver stated in disgust. "Men like Hawk Daily sicken me. They are arrogant and prideful, crude and plain stupid. You could do much better than that man, Ms. Bates."

Nikki looked up into Oliver's eyes. She knew she had to protect Hawk from the deadly man. "Hawk's okay. I'm not planning to marry the guy or anything. Truth is...I want to use Hawk to make my ex-husband jealous."

Oliver grinned. "I see," he stated in a delighted voice. "How wonderful a plan."

Nikki shrugged her shoulders. "I have to be patient. My husband is going to visit at Thanksgiving when my son comes back for his college break. I have until then to make it appear that Hawk and I are really serious. I like Hawk...he's a good man, and I hate to play with his heart, but I want my husband back."

"Excellent," Oliver said, not realizing that Nikki was manipulating him. "I assumed you despised your ex-husband."

"Hearts never stop loving," Nikki sighed and focused on the file in her hands.

"Perhaps," Oliver agreed.

Nikki felt a shiver crawl down her spine. Bracing herself, she eased forward with extreme caution. "Could I dare to ask you who you worked for, Mr. Bates?"

"You could," Oliver replied. "I will make it very simple for you, if you wish."

"Nothing is simple, but please try."

"I worked for the Center for Disease Control," Oliver explained. "My position will not be revealed, but I will state that I was a very powerful man. Early last year, I came to realize that my services at the Center were being questioned by a certain group of people in Washington."

"In other words, you were about to be eliminated," Nikki said.

"Yes," Oliver replied.

"I never had any dealings with the Center for Disease Control," Nikki admitted. "I'm afraid I'm not educated in that department, but I suppose you must have dealt with some very deadly diseases."

"Not dealt with...created," Oliver corrected Nikki. "Before my services were terminated, I made certain, shall I say, deals to obtain certain...items."

"I don't need to hear that," Nikki scolded him. "My job is to find a killer and clear myself of a murder. I just needed to know who you worked for to help me. It seems that if you were going to be eliminated by force, then it's possible that the person who killed your wife was sent to kill you. Now that I think about it, I'm sure of that."

Oliver sat quietly for a minute. "Perhaps," he finally answered in a disappointed tone. "I will leave you alone, now, Ms. Bates. I will be in touch tomorrow."

Nikki didn't say anything in reply. She watched the man put on his coat and hat and leave the room. "The games we play," Nikki whispered. "Okay, Jane Bates, you may not be in these files, but your parents might be. All I have to do is locate them while making Oliver think I'm searching for your killer. At least Oliver showed up on time and took the bait."

9

Rolling up her dress sleeves, Nikki went to work. Going through file after file, Nikki searched through one record after the next with a determined mind. When Hawk walked into the records room, she barely noticed. "Hungry?" he asked, examining all the files scattered across the sitting table.

"Huh? Oh, hi, Hawk," Nikki said wearily.

Hawk closed the door behind him, shook the brown coat he was wearing, and then ran his hands through his damp hair. "How are things here?"

"Oliver showed up like I expected. He was actually waiting for me," Nikki explained and began rubbing her neck. "I managed to squeeze some juice from that lemon, but not much. I have to admit, I was terrified the whole time. That man has done something awful to me and I don't know what. But I will. Until I do, I have to play his sick game."

Hawk walked over to Nikki and began massaging her

shoulders. "I did some digging for you, Nikki. Oliver Bates worked for—"

"The CDC, yeah, I got that much from him," Nikki said.

Hawk nodded. "The man was in charge of the Contagious Diseases Research department. Mr. Oliver Bates began his career with the CDC after leaving the Navy in 1976. Now here's the kicker. Are you ready?"

"Oliver Bates was originally assigned to the Vermont CDC, not the Atlanta CDC," Nikki told Hawk, "and that's how he met his wife, Jane, who is from Maple Hills."

Hawk sighed. "Well, you popped my balloon."

"Not really," Nikki explained. "I've been searching for confirmation of my theory. I'm trying to locate Jane's parents to confirm that she once lived in Maple Hills. It would help if I had the woman's maiden name."

Hawk beamed. "Funnel," he announced proudly.

Nikki turned in her seat and looked up into his eyes. "You've been on the job," she said, impressed.

"My fingers are more exhausted than my mind," he admitted.

Nikki smiled. "You're great." Standing up, she ran to a filing cabinet and pulled out a property tax file that belonged to a man named Lionel Funnel. "I've got an address."

"So do I," Hawk said, "and a graveyard. Nikki, you know Jane Funnel's parents are dead by now, don't you?"

"Oh, of course," Nikki said, "but I also want to see who is living in her old home."

"The house you're looking for is owned by a local

rental company," Hawk explained. "After lunch, I was going to find out if anyone was renting the house."

"My thoughts exactly," Nikki said and turned to face Hawk. "I believe Mr. Oliver Bates may be the current resident, Hawk."

Hawk patted the gun hidden under his coat. "Yep," he said.

Nikki looked past Hawk toward the table. "Thanks for your help, Hawk. I don't know why I didn't call you to begin with. Silly of me, really, to make all this mess when a simple phone call could have saved me time and trouble."

"Maybe you just needed time to think," Hawk suggested. "When my mind is tangling with a problem, I become distracted, too, and end up going around my elbow to get to my thumb."

"I guess," Nikki said. "Help me put these files away, and we'll go have lunch."

"Lidia and Tori are waiting at the diner for us," Hawk said as he began helping her clear the files.

Nikki suddenly stopped and looked at Hawk. She froze as her mind swung a bright, shiny object in front of her eyes. Only this time, the object was shaped like a needle. "Hawk?"

"Are you okay?" Hawk asked, alarmed.

"I..." Nikki struggled to speak, "I..."

"Sit down."

Nikki took Hawk's arm and sat.

"Want some water?"

"No, I'm..." Nikki closed her eyes. As she did, she saw herself standing in a gray light. Suddenly, a hand appeared and jabbed a needle into her neck. Nikki jerked and threw her eyes open.

"What is it?" Hawk asked, watching Nikki begin to breathe in short, panicked gasps as her eyes grew wide with fear.

"I'm not sure," Nikki whispered. "Please, let's leave. I need some fresh air."

Hawk helped Nikki stand up. With shaky hands, she put on her coat and ski cap. "Ready?" Hawk asked.

Nikki nodded. "And a little hungry. Maybe some food will help."

As Nikki walked out of the records room, she walked away from certain memories that were whispering into her mind, breaking away from frozen screams and melting into a nightmare.

10

A fter lunch, Nikki and Hawk drove to the rental house while Lidia and Tori headed back to the police station. "Weather is getting worse," Hawk said, leaning forward in the driver's seat.

Nikki listened to the screaming winds lashing sleet against the jeep. "I trust your driving. I do not trust icy roads," she told Hawk in a worried voice.

"Good thing the rental house is right here in town," Hawk replied. "There's no way we could have driven out into the country. I'm not even sure we're going to make it back to your cabin tonight. We may have to pitch a tent in my office."

Nikki braced herself as the jeep slid to a stop at a four-way intersection. The business district was now a block behind her. Cozy, warm townhomes stood before her, lining comfortable streets that any writer would imagine with delight. "Keep going," Nikki urged Hawk even though her heart was running laps.

Hawk looked to his left and then to his right. "Ice is

sticking to the power lines. My guess is this part of town will lose power before morning. Your cabin could be without power by now, too."

"One problem at a time," Nikki begged him. "First, let's drive by the rental home."

Hawk nodded and eased through the four-way stop. "The house isn't far. I bet ten bucks that's how Oliver Bates vanished from sight the other day. All he had to do was cut through a side street and wander off toward the rental house."

Nikki looked to her left as Hawk drove past a cute brick house. Smoke was rising from a stone chimney attached to the side of the house. Instead of imagining loving families gathered around a blazing fire, sharing stories, drinking hot chocolate, and eating popcorn, Nikki saw a dying woman struggling to crawl across a bedroom floor toward her. *Nikki...get help...Nikki, call for...help. Nikki...*

"Nikki?" Hawk asked.

"Huh?" She jumped in her seat.

"I said we're one street away from the rental house."

"Oh, okay. Drive slowly."

Hawk glanced at Nikki. Her face was pale, and her eyes were filled with horror and fear. "I wish I could walk inside your mind and save you from whatever monster is chasing you."

"Me, too," Nikki replied, her voice shaky.

Hawk slid the jeep to a stop at a second four-way stop. "There," he said and pointed to a little yellow house sitting on the right-hand corner of Pine Street. Nikki leaned forward and studied it. "I see lights on."

"Me, too," Hawk said, fixing his eyes on a gray, two-door car sitting in the driveway. I'm going to turn right, ease past the house, and get a look at the tag on that car."

Nikki drew in a deep breath. "Okay, let's go."

Inside the house, Oliver Bates was taking a hot shower. Having caught a chill from the icy weather, he feared that he might come down with a cold. Soaking up the hot steam, he was focused on his health and was completely unaware that Nikki and Hawk had located his hideout.

After his shower, Oliver took two Vitamin C pills, drank three cups of hot honey water, and settled down into an armchair with his laptop and waited for Nikki to return to her cabin. "I must make you more aware of the true killer," he whispered hideously. "The true killer is out there, Ms. Bates. Tick-tock, the sand is running out...for both you and me. We must hurry and play."

Back at the police station, Nikki walked into Hawk's office and plopped down in a cushioned chair in front of his desk. "Hey, guys," Nikki said in an exhausted voice.

Lidia and Tori were sitting in two chairs placed next to the window. "There is no way we're driving home tonight," Tori said, looking out the office window into the deep gray, icy day.

"I agree," Lidia confirmed. "And this wind, my goodness, I've never seen it this strong."

"Me neither," Hawk agreed, walking into his office and closing the door. "Okay, Nikki, I ran the tag."

"And?" Nikki asked anxiously.

"The car belongs to a rental company in New Jersey," Hawk explained, walking to his desk and sitting down.

"Oliver can't use credit cards," Nikki said, "and you need a credit card to rent a car."

"Not at Anywhere, Anytime Car Rental Service," Hawk told her. "You can rent a car with cash just as long as you pay the cash deposit."

"Surely this company would have taken a copy of Bates' driver's license," Nikki mused.

"Maybe, maybe not. I ran the company through the system, and let's just say the feedback is enough to make you cringe. Basically, the company rents lemons that aren't worth two cents."

"Okay, so Oliver got away with renting a lemon," Nikki replied in a tired voice, "but I'm sure he's not going to be driving a lemon for the rest of his life. Hawk, the man is a dangerous killer. He's not walking blind here. That man has probably purchased a new vehicle and home on a tropical island somewhere."

Hawk crossed his ankle over his left knee. "With the Canadian border right up the road, he can make a hasty escape, too. I have nothing to charge him with at this point, though," he muttered. "Sure, we found a few bread crumbs to stuff in our pockets today, but where does that leave us?"

"Well," Nikki said, attempting to sound positive, "let's count our bread crumbs. We know that Jane Bates was from Maple Hills and that Oliver Bates went to work at the CDC in Vermont after he left the navy. It's likely that he met Jane in Maple Hills somewhere along the line. Oliver was probably transferred to Atlanta, which explains how he ended up in Georgia." Nikki rubbed her eyes. "Jane was murdered and managed to scrawl a few lipstick letters on her bedroom floor, leaving behind some form of a clue. Oliver believes her killer lives in Maple Hills, but I'm not so sure. I believe the man is playing a game. I also believe he killed Mrs. Grove."

"I'm going to run the marriage license," Hawk told Nikki, "and find out where Bates married his wife. I'm also going to check with Atlanta and see what they have on Oliver and Jane. Maybe Atlanta might have a breadcrumb for us?"

"Good idea," Nikki agreed. "Also, Hawk, find out if Oliver went hiking in South America with someone...anyone. I have to believe he has a friend in his back pocket somewhere."

"I'll call a friend of mine in New York and see what he can come up with."

Nikki continued to rub her eyes. As she did, the image of a dead woman reappeared in her mind. *Nikki...call for help...help...help...* Nikki yanked her eyes open. "Oh my," she whimpered.

"What is it, honey?" Lidia asked and rushed over to Nikki.

Nikki looked up into Lidia's worried eyes. "Oh Lidia!" She began to cry and threw her face into Lidia's stomach. "It's so awful...I can see her!"

"Who?" Hawk asked.

Lidia placed her right hand on the back of Nikki's neck to comfort her. "Who, honey? Who do you see?"

"A dead woman, lying on a floor and begging me to call for help," Nikki cried.

Hawk looked at Lidia and then at Tori. Tori stood up and walked over to Lidia. "Is there anything I can do?" she asked worriedly.

Lidia shook her head. "I'm afraid not."

"I keep seeing this shiny object going back and forth in front of my eyes. And earlier today, I saw the object turn into a needle...and I saw a man stick the needle into my neck," Nikki explained through tears.

"Oh my," Lidia said and looked to Hawk for help.

Hawk rubbed his chin. "Nikki, look at me."

Nikki lifted her head and focused on Hawk. "Yes?" she asked and wiped at her tears.

"I think it's possible that somewhere down the line you were hypnotized. I think you realize that by now, too." Hawk stood up and walked to Nikki. Taking her hands, he looked softly into her tear-filled eyes. "I have an idea."

"I'm listening," Nikki promised.

"This may sound silly, so bear with me." Hawk drew in a deep breath. "When I was a cop in New York, I watched a doctor hypnotize a woman who witnessed a murder. The woman was so traumatized that her mind blocked out every detail of the murder. Needless to say, the doctor was able to help the woman bypass her trauma and remember what she had seen. I was pretty amazed because, well, I was skeptical about the whole hypnotism act."

"You want to hypnotize me?" Nikki asked Hawk.

Hawk nodded. "Your mind is leaking out what you

were programmed to forget," Hawk explained. "Sooner or later you're bound to remember everything that you have forgotten, but we don't have time to wait around."

"Isn't that kind of dangerous?" Tori asked, concerned. "Hawk, playing with someone's mind can cause a lot of harm. Are you really qualified to hypnotize someone?"

"Nope," Hawk said simply, keeping his eyes locked on Nikki, "and I probably never will be qualified, either."

"I want to remember," Nikki pleaded. "I need to remember. I think Oliver Bates killed his wife, Hawk. I know he killed Mrs. Grove. And now he's after me, playing some kind of sick game. The man is a dangerous killer...and he's set his sights on me, and I don't know why."

"Could it be because you saw him kill his wife?" Lidia asked Nikki. "How old is this weirdo?"

"Early seventies," Nikki answered.

"What age was he when his wife was murdered?"

"Forty-eight," Hawk told Lidia.

"So do the math...that would have put Nikki in her early twenties, right?" Lidia asked.

Nikki nodded. "I would have been twenty-one or twenty-two, I guess. I was in journalism school at that age."

A bell went off in Hawk's mind. "Nikki, what if Oliver's wife called you to her home to report something to you concerning her husband? And what if Oliver found out and killed his wife before she could tell you? And what if you walked in and found the woman dying on her bedroom floor? And," Hawk finished, "what if Oliver appeared and injected you with something and then programmed your mind to forget?"

"It's... possible," Nikki answered Hawk, "but those are a lot of 'what if's. I didn't even know Jane Bates."

"Maybe you did, and you just don't remember it," Hawk said. "You're seeing this woman in your mind because you're remembering her. And if you're remembering her, then you knew her somehow."

"Hawk is right," Lidia told Nikki.

"Yeah, I think he is," Tori added. "Hawk, we trust you."

Hawk bit down on his lower lip. "Nikki?"

Nikki stared into Hawk's eyes. "I have to know. I have to defeat Oliver Bates."

"Okay," Hawk said and let go of Nikki's hands. Rubbing his neck, he studied his office. "Tori, close the blinds. Nikki, pull a chair into the middle of the room."

Nikki became very nervous. She watched Hawk hurry to his computer as she pulled a chair into the middle of the office. Hawk jumped online and brought up a website that played relaxing piano music. "That should do it," he said as a soft, soothing melody floated into the air. "Nikki, sit down. Lidia, Tori, stand outside my office door, and don't let anyone disturb us."

"Come on," Lidia said and grabbed Tori's hand.

"You can do this," Tori told Nikki and hugged her neck.

Hawk waited until Lidia and Tori had left his office before he reached into his front pocket and pulled out a gold pocket watch. "This watch belonged to my dad," he told Nikki.

Nikki stared at the watch as the winds howled and screamed outside. "Hawk, are you sure you can do this?"

Hawk walked to Nikki, bent down, and gently kissed her lips. "Nikki, all I'm sure of is that I love you."

Nikki felt her heart reach out for Hawk. She gently touched his caring face. "Okay, my knight in shining armor, hypnotize me."

Hawk smiled. "Mind if I hypnotize you to love me forever?" he asked.

"I already do," Nikki promised and drew in a deep breath. "I'm ready."

Hawk grew silent. He listened to the ice hit the office window for a few seconds. "Okay, Nikki, here we go," he said in a low whisper and dropped the gold pocket watch down in front of Nikki's eyes.

11

Oliver Bates became furious when Nikki knocked on the front door of the house his wife had grown up in. "May I come in?" Nikki asked, standing on the small, ice-covered front porch as the winds howled all around her.

"You're a very sneaky person, now aren't you?" Oliver growled. Looking past Nikki into the dark night, he searched for any sign that Nikki had arrived with back-up. Instead, he saw her SUV parked in the driveway next to the rental car. "Inside," he commanded.

Nikki stepped into a small, warm foyer covered with pale yellow wallpaper. "I have some news for you," she told Oliver, shaking the ice off her coat. "I've found the killer."

"Have you now?"

Nikki studied the old man. He was wearing a gray jogging outfit and thick, wool socks. Suddenly he appeared very old and very weak in Nikki's eyes. But, Nikki quickly warned herself, the body may look old, yet the mind was still extremely deadly. "I won't take too much of your time tonight," Nikki told Oliver. "I need to get home as soon as possible."

"Yes, the weather is much worse," he stated, forcing his voice to sound firm and under control. "How did you find out my location? First, answer me that."

"You didn't hide yourself very well," Nikki replied, a hint of mock disappointment in her voice. "Any amateur sleuth could have found you, Mr. Bates."

Nikki's response slapped Oliver across his face. "Do not test me, Ms. Bates, do you understand me?" he snarled.

"Listen," Nikki said, sidestepping the threat, "I've located a man who lived in Atlanta at the time your wife was murdered. He has to be the killer. I'm going to speak with him tomorrow. I need you to come with me."

Oliver locked eyes with Nikki and attempted to reach into her mind. "Is that so?"

"Yes," Nikki answered. "Mr. Bates, you twisted my arm and forced me to track down the person who killed your wife. I have completed my duty as you asked, assuming Mr. Purry is our man, that is. I am taking a blind leap of faith here. I assume you are not playing games with me and that you really want to find the killer."

"And the killer could be this...Mr. Purry?" Oliver asked.

"Charlie Purry," Nikki explained, repeating the false name. "The man lived in Atlanta and ran an antique shop. He left Atlanta soon after your wife was killed. Before Mr. Purry left Atlanta, he drew the attention of the police, who began investigating him for selling stolen goods. My guess is this man somehow knew your wife, Mr. Bates, and your wife knew about his crooked business. He must have killed Jane to keep her silent."

"I see," Oliver said coldly. "Well, perhaps we should pay this Mr. Purry a visit."

"Good. Meet me at my store at noon tomorrow. The weatherman isn't forecasting good weather anytime soon, so dress warmly."

"Of course," Oliver assured her. "Now, hurry home."

"I'll be driving very slowly and very carefully," Nikki replied and opened the front door. "Tomorrow at noon. And please, Mr. Bates, I request that you refrain from violence. We're just going to speak with Mr. Purry and ask some questions."

"Of course," Oliver replied and bid Nikki a safe trip home. "Tomorrow, Nikki Bates, you will find out who Mrs. Grove's real killer is. I'm pleased that you're playing my game, but the time has come to end it." He slammed the front door shut then grumbled, "Tomorrow I will help you remember what I programmed you to forget. You will remember all the agony you caused me. When I am finished, you will be begging me for mercy. Oh yes, tomorrow you will know the truth, Nikki Bates."

Nikki hurried to her SUV, slipping and sliding on the ice. She carefully climbed up into the driver's seat. "The stage is set," she whispered to Hawk.

Keeping his head down in the back seat, Hawk waited until Nikki maneuvered away from the house and then crawled into the front seat and buckled up. "Are you sure that snake will take the bait?"

"Right now," Nikki told Hawk as she drove slowly back toward town, "Oliver Bates' mind is running in a hundred different directions. The one fact he is sure of is that I am lying to him. Tomorrow, he'll come at me with full force."

"How do you know this?" Hawk asked.

Nikki eased her SUV up to a stop sign. "Hawk, I saw the man kill his wife. I saw the man inject me with some kind of hypnotic serum. I saw the man inject me again with the same serum before I left Atlanta. He programmed me to relocate to Maple Hills, Vermont. Why? Because he intended to kill me. But first, he wanted to play his sick little game."

"Because you told Oliver Bates' wife you were smarter than her husband before he killed the poor woman, and he overheard you," Hawk said.

Nikki nodded. "I was young and full of myself back then, Hawk. I thought for sure I could take down Oliver Bates with one single hit. When Jane Bates called me on the night of August 2nd, she was very scared. She told me Oliver had threatened to kill her, and she needed my help." Nikki said. "Jane Bates was going to make a deal with me—my help in exchange for information that could destroy Oliver."

"But he got to his wife first."

"Yes," Nikki said, remembering a stormy night in Atlanta. "I remember driving to their house, a large, two-story Victorian home in a wealthy neighborhood. It was dark, and a horrible storm was lashing the city. I parked my car a few houses down and jogged up to Jane's house."

"You two were friends at this point?"

"Kinda," Nikki explained. "I remember Oliver always being a cold fish and Jane being a shy and timid woman. I really didn't know them very well. Honestly, I can't remember how I even met Jane. Anyway, I made my way to the house, sneaked around to the back door, and found the spare key Jane had told me about." Nikki leaned forward on the steering wheel in order to see the road more clearly.

"What then?" Hawk asked.

"I remember I was wearing a green dress and tennis shoes. I was soaking wet by the time I unlocked the kitchen door and entered. My shoes squeaked on the tile floor...a white tile floor. I took them off and set them down beside the back door." Nikki lowered her voice. "The house was so silent...ominous. I knew something was wrong."

"Keep going," Hawk pressed Nikki.

"The kitchen was dark and full of shadows. Lightning was flashing outside, and then it thundered. That's when I heard Jane scream. I had a small pistol hidden in a green backpack I was carrying on my shoulders. The backpack had my notebooks, pens, a tape recorder...also a bottle of water and some candy bars. I took out the pistol and ran up the back stairs. I remember how the carpet felt under my bare feet."

Nikki drove her SUV into town and stopped in front of her chocolate store. "I made my way down a lovely hallway filled with antiques and beautiful paintings to a door that was pushed halfway open, and then..."

"And then what?"

"I eased the door open and saw Oliver Bates standing over his wife with a knife."

"That's when the woman began calling out to you for help."

"Yes," Nikki said, staring through the storm at her shop. "Hawk, I froze...I didn't know what to do. All I remember is running, running back down the hallway, and then I felt a horrible pain strike the side of my neck, and everything went dark."

"While Oliver Bates was dealing with you, his wife managed to scribble a few lipstick letters on her bedroom floor," Hawk continued the narrative. "But before Oliver could erase them, the police arrived. A neighbor reported seeing a suspicious person sneaking around outside the house and called the police. That sneaky person was you."

Nikki closed her eyes. "Years later, my memory of that night began to make an appearance in my mind," Nikki said, keeping her eyes closed. "I wasn't certain what storm was brewing in my mind...I kept seeing flashes of Jane Bates lying dead on her bedroom floor, the silver watch Oliver used to hypnotize me, and the needle...awful images. But Hawk, I didn't remember that Oliver was the killer. I made a horrible mistake and phoned him one day and explained to him what was happening to me. Like a fool, I asked for his help. After all, the man was my daddy's adopted brother."

"Oliver Bates met you in your home," Hawk said in a low voice as his eyes studied the dark storm, "and injected you with the same serum he injected you with the night he killed his wife. He programmed you to move to Maple Hills."

"To put me on ice, so to speak," Nikki whispered. "I remember him telling me that he would play a final game with me and prove that he was the chess master, and I was nothing more than a mere pawn."

"So he kills Mrs. Grove and pushes you into a tight corner while sending you out to find a false killer."

"Waiting until I figured out that he was the real killer, and when I did, he would be waiting for me...but not to kill me," Nikki finished. "Oliver Bates has a design for me. In the end, he wants me to rot in prison...and have plenty of time to torture myself about how he outsmarted me."

"The evidence he promised to give you concerning Mrs. Grove is evidence that he will send to the State Police," Hawk said and shook his head. "Evidence that will lead to your conviction."

"I'm afraid so," Nikki agreed. "Hawk, I believe Oliver Bates hypnotized Mrs. Grove before he killed her and programmed her to make a fake accusation, claiming that I threatened to kill her."

"I was thinking something along those lines," Hawk replied. "What's important is that you remember now."

"I wish I didn't," Nikki said. Turning to face him, she looked into his worried face. "You did a wonderful job hypnotizing me, Hawk. I'm very grateful, even though I will have to live with these horrible memories now. But we have bullets to fire at Oliver Bates, and that's more important than losing a few nights of sleep."

"We're banking on this psycho believing that you're lying to him," Hawk said and shook his head again.

"I have to make Oliver think I'm playing his game. The man is mentally disturbed, Hawk. He believes he's controlling me and that he's in charge of the game. Tomorrow it'll all be over."

Hawk nodded toward the street. "Let's get back to your cabin and continue the game," he said.

"Okay." Nikki got her SUV moving through the ice and wind. Hawk grew silent and didn't speak again until Nikki had safely pulled the SUV into the driveway leading up to her cabin. "Hawk, what are you thinking?" Nikki asked.

"Will you leave Maple Hills now?" he asked in a low whisper. "Now that you know the truth?"

Nikki leaned over and kissed him. "Out of every rock comes a diamond." She smiled into his eyes. "You're my home, Lidia and Tori are my home, Maple Hills is my home. I'm not going anywhere, tiger."

Hawk smiled and kissed her. "Good, because if you ever try to leave, I will handcuff you to my office door. Come on, let's get inside."

12

Tori and Lidia were sitting at the kitchen table. When they saw Nikki and Hawk rush through the back door, they both let out sighs of relief. "We were thinking the worst."

"We're all safe, and that's what matters," Nikki said, shaking the ice off her coat. "Did Mr. Purry call?"

"No," Tori said in a convincing voice.

From across town, Oliver was watching every move Nikki made and listening to her every word. "Perhaps you did find someone whom you actually think is the killer?" Oliver mused, staring at his laptop with a cup of honey water in his hand.

"It's vital that Mr. Purry shows up," Nikki told Tori. She took off her coat and handed it to Hawk.

"Should we be talking about this...with you-know-who listening?" Lidia asked, jumping into character.

"I've already paid Oliver Bates a visit and told him about Mr. Purry," Nikki answered and walked to the kitchen counter. "I'll make some coffee."

Hawk took off his coat. "I don't approve of your method, Nikki. I'm a cop, after all," he said and hung up his and Nikki's coats on the wooden coat rack standing next to the back door.

"It's the only way to find the person who killed Mrs. Grove," Nikki told Hawk in a stern voice. "Listen, Hawk, you're a great guy and all, but don't stand in my way, okay? My son's life is in jeopardy. I'll do what Oliver Bates asked me to do and then get rid of him."

"Are you sure he'll go away?" Lidia asked worriedly.

Nikki worked on making the coffee. "I have my memory back," Nikki informed Lidia. "I know Oliver Bates killed his wife. I know he hypnotized me. If he refuses to hold up his end of the bargain, then I'll toss this case into Hawk's lap and let him arrest the man and—" Nikki stopped talking and threw her hands over her mouth. Hawk, Lidia, and Tori all stared at her, stunned. "I didn't mean...it slipped...I..."

Oliver slowly set down the cup of honey water he was holding and grinned. "So you remember, do you?"

"Maybe he didn't hear?" Lidia murmured, terrified.

Nikki lowered her hands. "He heard...he will be calling me any minute now," she whispered.

"Yes, I shall," Oliver smiled deviously and picked up his cell phone and dialed Nikki's home number.

The phone rang on cue. Nikki answered the call with shaky hands. "You heard me, didn't you?"

"So, you remember?"

"Listen to me," Nikki said in a terrified voice, "I found someone on whom you can pin Jane's murder, Oliver. Please, take him and leave Maple Hills. Do whatever you want with the man, I don't care. Just give me the evidence I need to clear my name and leave me and my son alone."

"What do you remember, Nikki?" Oliver asked in a creepy whisper. "Do you remember telling my wife that you were a brilliant woman who was going to outsmart the fox? Oh yes, you told Jane those very words. I remember hearing them. I was standing outside the bedroom door when you spoke those words. But even worse, you caused my wife to turn on me. I loved my wife, Nikki, and you transformed her into my enemy."

"I'm sorry," Nikki told Oliver and began allowing a fake cry to leave her lips. "Oliver, I was young and stupid. I swear I will not tell the police anything. Please..."

Oliver stared at Nikki's face on his laptop screen. "Please, what?"

"Play my game," Nikki begged. "Hawk and I created a false killer for you. You can have Mr. Purry in exchange for the evidence I need. I know you killed your wife, but...who is going to believe me? Even if Hawk arrested you, what charges could he hold you on? Everything is merely circumstantial. I didn't mean to betray you, but it was the only way."

"I see," Oliver said in a sick, pleased voice. "I'm impressed, Nikki. You played the game I created very well in the short time frame I allowed. For a minute, I was concerned that you were going to be no challenge to me."

"Oliver...what will...what I mean is, will you make a bargain with me?" Nikki pleaded.

"Of course," Oliver lied, "as long as you admit that the fox just ate the last chicken."

"Yes, yes, okay," Nikki nearly screamed, "you

outsmarted me! Is that what you want to hear? You are the chess master, and I'm merely a pawn!"

Oliver grinned. "What sweet words, Ms. Bates. I appreciate your honesty. Now, bring this Mr. Purry tomorrow at our set time, and I will exchange him for the evidence you need."

"No games?" Nikki asked.

"The game is over," Oliver lied. "I won. But let me give you a warning, Nikki."

"A warning?"

"I will retain certain evidence. If you ever try to speak to the police—the real police, and not the cowboy standing next to the back door—I will send the evidence forward. You may threaten to make my face known on your pathetic social media platforms, but I assure you, you will be the one gracing the 'Most Wanted' posters across this country."

"No games, I promise," Nikki said. "I'll be at my store at noon with Mr. Purry."

"I look forward to our meeting," Oliver replied and ended the call.

Nikki quickly pretended to dial a number and slammed the phone up against her ear. "Pick up...pick up," she said in a nervous, loud voice. "Mr. Purry, thank goodness, I was afraid you might not be home... Oh yes, where would you be on a night like this? Listen, Mr. Purry, I need to confirm that you are still going to meet me at my store tomorrow at noon... Yes, I know the weather is bad, and the roads are hazardous...Yes, I know your back hurts, but Mr. Purry, I have some very important information regarding your past that you need to know about...No, this isn't blackmail; please, just meet me at my store...Yes, at noon...Okay, I'll see you then." Nikki hung up the phone and looked at Hawk. "Make sure no cops are around my store at noon, Hawk."

"I could lose my job and my pension," Hawk fussed. "I should have never agreed to this."

"You're in too deep now," Tori snapped at him. "You have to help Nikki."

"Please," Lidia begged Hawk. "Help her."

"Okay, okay," Hawk surrendered, "I'll keep the local boys busy." He rubbed the back of his neck and shook his head. "I'm going for a shower."

Nikki watched Hawk leave the kitchen. She looked at Lidia and Tori. "Coffee anyone?" They both raised their hands.

13

T he following morning, Nikki pretended to sneak out of her cabin without anyone seeing. Wearing a thick white coat over a brown wool turtleneck dress, she hoped her appearance showed a certain style and confidence. Of course, the heavy boots on her feet and the white ski cap made her feel clumsy and silly, but that didn't matter, Nikki thought. She slipped and slid across the icy driveway to her SUV as powerful winds howled into her face. The world was white with ice, but at least the storm had passed during the night, leaving only the winds as an afterthought. Still, the ice was dangerous, and she had to drive with extreme caution.

As Nikki climbed into her SUV and got the heat going, Oliver studied the screen on his laptop. Hawk was on Nikki's living room couch, asleep. Tori and Lidia were both asleep in the guest bedroom. "Up so early and leaving without the cowboy," Oliver said and took a sip of coffee instead of honey water. "What are you up to? Perhaps I should take a stroll up to your store."

Nikki counted on Oliver seeing her sneak out of the cabin. As she backed out of the driveway, her mind began to race. "Calm down," she whispered. "You're in control of this game. You can do this, girl. You're Nikki Bates and—"

"And you make some really good chocolates."

Nikki screamed and slammed on the brakes. The SUV skidded to a stop. Chief Daily straightened up from the back seat. "Mr. Purry at your service."

"Oh, Chief Daily," Nikki said, terrified, and then laughed. "You scared me!"

Chief Daily crawled into the front seat. "Okay, here's how I have the board arranged. The FBI is using the same satellite to monitor Oliver Bates' movements that he's been using to watch yours. But we have to be careful, Nikki. The man has stolen a very deadly virus. He also stole an equally deadly chemical that if used in a smoke form, can put an entire city block to sleep...for good."

"The same chemical found in my chocolate."

Chief Daily nodded. "Nikki, we have credible information that Oliver Bates is going to transfer his stolen substances to a known terrorist group in Canada. We have to stop him."

"I guess it was a good thing he decided to pay me a visit first," Nikki said.

"The man is mentally ill, Nikki, and very unstable. He was diagnosed with cancer last year. I guess he wants to go out with a bang."

"And destroy me in the process," Nikki sighed.

Chief Daily looked down at the cell phone he was holding. A map glowed on the screen. On the map, a little red dot was moving. "Bates is on the move. You better get us moving, too."

As Nikki drove toward town, Chief Daily reached into the back seat and grabbed a black backpack. Opening it, he pulled out a fake beard and wig. "The wig and beard along with this gray suit should make me look convincing."

"I hope so," Nikki said. "Chief Daily, you don't think Oliver Bates will release the virus he stole in Maple Hills, do you? He only wants to destroy my life."

"Who knows?" Chief Daily answered honestly. "A man in his mental state is capable of anything. But what I do know is that I'm glad you and I are on the same team."

Nikki smiled. "Me, too."

Nikki parked her SUV in front of her store and carefully climbed out. Chief Daily followed suit, fussing the entire time. "You didn't need to come to my home!" he complained.

"I needed to make sure you were going to keep your word," Nikki replied. "Please, Mr. Purry, let's talk inside my store. It's freezing out here."

Chief Daily glanced around the ice-covered downtown district. "Yes, fine," he agreed. "You can make me a cup of coffee."

Already standing inside Nikki's chocolate shop, Oliver Bates watched Nikki help an older gentleman up an icy sidewalk toward the front door. "Hello, Mr. Purry," he whispered and dropped back into the shadows.

Nikki reached into her coat pocket and drew out the store keys. With cold hands, she unlocked the front door and moved aside. "After you, Mr. Purry."

Chief Daily stepped into the store, found the light switch, and flipped it on. As soon as the lights pushed the darkness away, Oliver appeared with a pistol in his right hand. "Close the door, Nikki," he ordered.

Nikki looked at the pistol and slowly closed and locked the front door. "Here he is, Oliver."

"What is this all about?" Chief Daily asked in an angry voice. "Who are you? And how dare you aim a gun at me?"

"You're early," Oliver told Nikki, ignoring Chief Daily.

"The roads are dangerous, and I needed to make a side stop and gather up Mr. Purry," Nikki explained.

"Who are you?" Chief Daily demanded, locking eyes with Oliver. "What is this all about?" Spinning around to face Nikki, he threw a finger into her face. "Is this some kind of joke, Ms. Bates? Because I am not amused."

"Please, Mr. Purry, just speak with Mr. Bates," Nikki begged.

Oliver shook his head at Nikki. "Nikki, did you really believe I would accept this awful man in exchange for justice?"

"What do you mean?" Nikki asked, alarmed. "Oliver, we made a deal."

"No, Nikki, you made a deal," Oliver grinned. "Now you will be locked away in prison for two murders instead of one."

"What do you mean?"

Oliver took his left hand and reached into his coat

pocket and extracted a syringe. "Inject this serum into Mr. Purry's neck, Ms. Bates, at once," he ordered.

"But we made a deal! I..." Nikki stumbled. "Oliver, I swear, I won't tell anyone you killed your wife. I promise."

Oliver rolled his eyes. "Nikki, Nikki, Nikki, please don't insult yourself in such a demeaning manner. As you can clearly see, I'm in control. I was in control the night I murdered my wife and disposed of your memory, and I'm in control now."

"You killed your wife?" Chief Daily asked in a shocked voice.

Oliver rolled his eyes again. "Are you deaf?" he asked.

"Many years ago, this man murdered his wife in Atlanta, Georgia," Nikki told Chief Daily, pretending to act weak and scared.

"I injected my wife with the same chemical I used to disable and murder Mrs. Grove," Oliver confessed proudly. "But Jane was a fighter and required more...force."

"I saw the murder," Nikki told Chief Daily, "but before I could escape, this man captured me and injected me with the same serum he wants me to inject you with."

"Oh yes," Oliver hissed as he breathed in the scent of delicious chocolate, "this serum is a very dear friend. It allows me to control the minds of my victims. For example," Oliver motioned toward the front counter with his eyes, "press play on that tape recorder, Nikki."

Hesitantly, Nikki walked to the front counter and pressed play on a small, black tape recorder. The voice of Mrs. Grove began screaming, "No! Nikki, don't...don't hurt me...no..."

And then, to Nikki's horror, she heard her own voice yell, "I'm going to kill you!"

"You see," Oliver said, pleased, "I control everyone."

"My voice—I sounded much younger," Nikki told Oliver.

"You, Nikki, are going to prison for the murder of my wife and Mrs. Grove."

"What about Mr. Purry?" Nikki asked.

Oliver's face became very displeased. "Mr. Purry will come with me and serve an entirely different purpose."

Chief Daily looked at Nikki. The time to act had come. "I'm leaving at once," he said and marched toward the front door. With his back turned toward Oliver, he reached into his jacket and pulled a gun from a hidden shoulder holster. "Freeze!" Chief Daily yelled, spinning around. But before he could say anything else, Oliver fired, and the shot hit Chief Daily in the chest.

"No!" Nikki yelled as the chief crashed down onto the floor. "You monster!"

Oliver pointed his gun at Nikki. "You betrayed me!" he hissed. "I believed that man was really who you said he was!"

Nikki ran to Chief Daily and squatted down beside him. "No," she cried.

"Stand up," Oliver ordered Nikki and slung the syringe at her. "Inject the syringe into your neck immediately."

"You monster!" Nikki yelled again.

"Stand up now, or I will make your son forget you ever existed, Nikki Bates," Oliver warned.

Nikki stood up. "Okay, okay..." she said and picked up

the syringe. Drawing in a deep breath, she slid the needle into the side of her neck. Slowly, she became very still and very mute.

"Very good," Oliver said, pleased. Putting his gun away, he walked over to Nikki. Waving his hands in front of her eyes, he tested her reactions. "Nikki?" She didn't respond. "Excellent." He took her hand, walked her into the back office, sat her down in a chair, and then journeyed back into the store.

Nikki glanced at the office door. "Hawk, the fake skin on my neck protected me," she whispered, "but he shot your dad. I think his bulletproof vest stopped the bullet, but I'm not sure." Hearing movement, Nikki looked forward and pretended to be in a hypnotic daze.

Oliver pushed open the office door. With tremendous effort, he pulled Chief Daily's body into the office. "Now," he said, breathing hard, "it's time to end this game." Standing in front of Nikki, he reached into his pocket and drew out a silver pocket watch and began swinging the item back and forth in front of Nikki's eyes. In an instant, Nikki blinked, reached out, and grabbed Oliver's wrists. "What…no!" Oliver yelled, startled.

Nikki lunged to her feet, released her right hand, balled it into a tight fist, and punched Oliver as hard as she could in the face. He stumbled backward, tripped over Chief Daily's body, and fell down onto the floor. "The games we play always end," Nikki told him.

Dazed and hurt, Oliver struggled to look up at Nikki. With weak hands, he tried to retrieve his gun, but Chief Daily grabbed his hand before he could. "No, you don't," Chief Daily said in a pained voice.

"You're alive!" Nikki cried.

Before Oliver could understand what was happening, Hawk rushed into the office with his gun drawn. When he saw Oliver lying next to Chief Daily, he ran to the man and slapped handcuffs on him. "You're under arrest."

"Am I?" Oliver asked wearily. "Perhaps the game is over," he said and looked at Nikki with deadly eyes, "but not for me."

"The virus?" Nikki exclaimed and pulled the fake skin off her neck and threw it down onto the floor.

Oliver stared at her. "So you are smarter than I assumed," he said, "but fake skin will not save you from my virus."

"Where is the virus?" Hawk demanded.

"By noon the town of Maple Hills will become one silent graveyard," Oliver informed Hawk. "You see, I don't like to lose. I figured if I somehow lost to Ms. Bates, I would still win in the end."

Chief Daily struggled to his feet and rubbed his chest. "Darn vest never works well."

"You're alive, Pop, be grateful," Hawk said.

"Yeah, but for how long?" Chief Daily asked worriedly. "Hawk, we need to begin evacuating everyone out of Maple Hills. We have less than..." Chief Daily checked his watch, "one hour."

Oliver laughed. "Run away, little rats, but you will never escape. You see, my virus is attached to a voice-controlled bomb. All I have to do is say the password and...well, perhaps people will receive more than a mere runny nose. Now, take these horrible handcuffs off me and

I will spare this miserable little town. And you, Nikki Bates, I will deal with you some other time."

Nikki marched up to Oliver and locked eyes with him. "Look into my eyes, Oliver, and listen carefully. If you release your virus, you will die. I will stand right here and watch you die, even if it means dying along with you. Today your sick game ends."

Oliver stared right back. "Set me free, or people will die, and you will be the one everyone will blame."

"So be it, just as long as you die," Nikki replied. "Hawk, Chief Daily, start evacuating the town. I will remain right here with this monster—this monster who killed an innocent woman who found out her husband was creating a deadly virus in the basement of their home. How much did you get paid to betray your country, Mr. Bates? Was it enough to kill your wife and forsake your career?"

"You will suffer," Oliver promised Nikki. "I will return for you. I control you."

"You no longer control anything! Your days of terrorizing people are over."

"Never," Oliver hissed in Nikki's face.

Nikki grinned. Reaching into the front pocket of Oliver's jacket, she pulled out a second syringe. "I assumed you came prepared with a back-up. Now, let's make you talk."

Oliver's eyes grew wide. "No, you mustn't...No!"

"Hawk, get ready to become an expert at hypnosis," Nikki said and jabbed the syringe into Oliver's neck. The last thing Oliver Bates would remember before waking up behind bars would be Nikki Bates' victorious face smiling at him.

"Son, do you think you can make this man talk?" Chief Daily asked.

"Only one way to find out," Hawk said and pulled his gold pocket watch out. "Okay," he said and drew in a deep breath, "here we go."

Outside, the winds continued to howl and scream as another storm front moved toward the sleepy little town of Maple Hills.

14

"So, you found the virus hidden in the car?" Lidia asked Nikki as she helped her slide a pretty brown couch out onto the floor of the chocolate shop. "Whew, this is hard work. Time for a break."

Nikki agreed and plopped down onto the couch. "We found the virus hidden in the trunk of the rental car, attached to a small fan. The bomb in the trunk was designed to pop the trunk open while igniting the fan at the same time. I hate to admit it, but it was a brilliant design," Nikki explained. Glancing down at the blue wool dress she was wearing, she smiled. "Hawk is taking me for a walk in the snow later."

Lidia looked at the front window. Heavy snow was falling, covering Maple Hills with a cozy, white blanket. "Herbert used to take me for walks in the snow," she sighed. "Maybe I can get that old coot to stir long enough to throw a snowball at a squirrel?"

Nikki laughed. "I'm sure you can!" She looked at Tori. "How's it going?"

"All set," Tori beamed. Carrying a wooden tray holding three white cups of hot coconut cocoa, she eased her way toward the couch from behind the front counter.

"Don't spill any on that pretty green dress," Lidia begged.

"And don't you spill a drop on that gorgeous pink sweater Nikki and I bought you," Tori smiled at Lidia.

Lidia looked down at her sweater. "I would never forgive myself if I did," she told them.

"You look beautiful," Tori exclaimed. "It's hot, be careful," she said, lowering the wooden tray down to the couch.

Nikki took her cup of hot chocolate and leaned back. Staring at the falling snow through the front window, she sighed happily. "After Hawk and Chief Daily left me alone with Oliver, I made sure to end his game."

"Do tell," Lidia said excitedly as she took her cup of hot chocolate off the wooden tray.

"Yes, tell us," Tori begged.

"The name Nikki Bates means absolutely nothing to Oliver now. Anytime anyone mentions my name to him, he will only remember falling off a very high cliff...which I made him believe was his worst fear."

"You're a very devious woman," Lidia teased.

"I have my son to protect," Nikki replied, keeping her eyes on the snow. "Oliver Bates no longer knows my son exists, either."

"You did well," Lidia congratulated Nikki. "You won the battle against a very deadly man and saved countless lives. Everyone in Maple Hills is grateful to you...except a few, who are moving away."

Nikki grew solemn. "The battle is won for now, but when will the next one arrive? When will the next criminal show up and throw pie in my face?"

Tori looked at Lidia. Lidia reached out with her left hand and patted Nikki's knee. "Honey, if and when the next bozo shows up, we'll have your back. We're a family, and family sticks together."

"That's right," Tori agreed.

Nikki smiled. "Thanks, girls. That means the world to me."

The front door opened, and Hawk walked in, paused, shook the snow off his brown coat, and then looked back over his shoulder. "Darn kids...Stop throwing snowballs at me!" he yelled.

Nikki giggled. "I see the 'Snowball Gang' has struck again."

"Brats," Hawk fussed and closed the front door. "Ready for lunch?"

"Ready for our walk in the snow, too," Nikki smiled.

"Not with those armed and dangerous brats outside," Hawk objected.

"Oh, Hawk, you aren't afraid of a bunch of nine-year-olds, are you?" Nikki asked.

"Yes, ma'am, I sure am," Hawk confessed. "Those kids have lethal aim. I got whapped in the back of the head four times before I could reach my jeep."

"Poor baby," Lidia told Hawk.

"Poor baby is right," Hawk replied and rubbed the back of his head. "Oh, by the way, I got some news I want to share."

"We're all ears," Nikki said and sipped her hot chocolate.

"Oliver Bates died of a heart attack earlier this morning. He was found dead in his cell, cold as ice," Hawk explained. "Some of the prison guards reported hearing him say your name and then scream, say your name again, and then scream. They said the man did that all night long."

Nikki smiled. "Well, now, at least Oliver Bates died knowing who really won the game. Justice is served. Let's go for our walk in the snow." Nikki giggled. "And don't worry, tiger, I'll protect you from those nine-year-old monsters lurking outside."

"Not funny, Nikki," Hawk groused. "Those brats hate me. Yesterday I got hit with a total of ten snowballs, and that was before lunch. I think they're trying to set a record or something."

Nikki stood up and walked to Hawk. Without saying a word, she stood up on her tippy-toes and kissed him. "Listen to me, Hawk Daily, I love you. Now take me for my walk in the snow. Afterward, we will walk to the diner, eat a nice lunch, and come back to the store."

"We need your back, big guy," Lidia told Hawk and tipped him a wink. "We have more furniture to move."

Tori smiled sweetly. "Don't worry, Hawk, Nikki will give you a discount on her chocolate for all your help."

Hawk looked into Nikki's beautiful eyes. "Come on, lady," he said in a loving voice, "let's go for that walk in the snow."

Nikki took Hawk's hand. "Someday you can put a ring on my finger," she promised Hawk as peace and happiness consumed her heart. Even though the future still held dark corners, Nikki felt prepared to face them with the man she loved and two friends who would always have her back.

Looking back at her chocolate store, Nikki drew in a deep breath of chocolate and closed her eyes. "Chocolate-covered mysteries on a snowy day...what a wonderful treat," she whispered happily. "What a sweet, wonderful treat after a hard day's work."

ABOUT THE AUTHOR

Wendy Meadows is the USA Today
bestselling author of many novels and
novellas, from cozy mysteries to
clean, sweet romances. Check out her
popular cozy mystery series
Sweetfern Harbor, Alaska Cozy and
Sweet Peach Bakery, just to name a few.

If you enjoyed this book, please take a few minutes to
leave a review. Authors truly appreciate this, and it helps
other readers decide if the book might be for them.
Thank you!

Get in touch with Wendy
www.wendymeadows.com

a amazon.com/author/wendymeadows

g goodreads.com/wendymeadows

BB bookbub.com/authors/wendy-meadows

f facebook.com/AuthorWendyMeadows

🐦 twitter.com/wmeadowscozy

Copyright © 2016 by Wendy Meadows

All rights reserved.

No part of this publication may be reproduced, distributed or transmitted in any form or by any means, without prior written permission.

This is a work of fiction. Names, characters, places, and incidents are a product of the author's imagination. Locales and public names are sometimes used for atmospheric purposes. Any resemblance to actual people, living or dead, or to businesses, companies, events, institutions, or locales is completely coincidental.